PUSHKIN CHILDREN'S

THE TUNNELS BELOW

'This is an impressive debut by Nadine Wild-Palmer... She has a tremendous imagination – I loved meeting the weird and wonderful creatures in this fantasy land'

The Times, Children's Book of the Week

'This hugely imaginative debut, with a brilliantly resourceful heroine, is one to look out for'

The Bookseller

'*The Tunnels Below* is a zippy and captivating read, full of cliffhanger chapter endings and inventive fantasy elements... Nadine Wild-Palmer's imagination is big and surprising and a joy to enter'

BookTrust

'A crazy adventure that skirts scary but is full of beautiful moments'

Scoop

D0710073

NADINE WILD-PALMER lives in South London. Her day job means she can be heard on Channel 4 as the voice-over artist announcing the programme schedules. Nadine is also a singer-songwriter and a poet, and she has worked as a children's librarian.

THE
TUNNELS
BELOW

Nadine Wild-Palmer

PUSHKIN CHILDREN'S

Pushkin Press
71–75 Shelton Street
London WC2H 9JQ

Copyright © 2019 Nadine Wild-Palmer

First published by Pushkin Press in 2019

3 5 7 9 8 6 4 2

ISBN 13: 978-1-78269-223-2

Author photo © Ty Faruki
Internal illustrations © Ellen Shi

Designed and typeset by Tetragon, London
Printed and bound by CPI Group (UK) Ltd, Croydon, CRO 4YY

www.pushkinpress.com

THE
TUNNELS
BELOW

A Marvellous Surprise

Have you ever woken up one morning and felt like everything has changed overnight? That's because it has. Cecilia Hudson-Gray woke up on the morning of her twelfth birthday to the gurgling sound of the radiators coming on. It was a frosty March morning and the windows wept with condensation as the heating kicked in to settle the cold. Cecilia looked out of her window and was met by two black eyes and a sharp black beak; she inhaled a large sniff and pulled her quilt around her tightly. One for sorrow she thought, remembering the first line of an old nursery rhyme. She watched the brave bird poking about on the window ledge, parading jauntily along like it was performing a circus act. As the magpie dipped forwards preparing for flight, Cecilia's brain also swooped into action as it occurred to her that there might be presents waiting downstairs! She leapt out of bed, her quilt flying out behind her like a cape, and thudded through the house like a rumble of thunder, followed by her sister, Hester, who must've heard Storm Cecilia passing.

"Happy Birthday," chimed her parents as Cecilia wedged herself in at the breakfast table.

"Thanks, guys!" she replied, pulling the sleeves of her pyjama top over her hands like mittens, shielding them from the chill of the morning and the heat of the hot cup of sweet tea in front of her. She picked it up and blew on it gently, tufts of steam rising off the surface.

"You'll stretch your sleeves and ruin your PJs doing that, you know," her dad warned, planting an apparently unwanted kiss on her mess of hair. Cecilia responded by brushing away the invisible imprint of the kiss as her sister entered the room.

Hester sidled up to Cecilia and whispered in her ear, "Nappy turd-day!" and sat down, smiling smugly.

Cecilia put down her cup and began a mocking slow-clap. "Very funny. How long did it take you to come up with that one... Fester?"

Hester refused a dignified response and stuck her finger in her nose, then reached out to wipe the fruits of her labour on Cecilia's arm.

"Daaaaad!" Cecilia wailed like a baby.

8

"Stop it, you two. Hester, it's not fair if you don't have enough to go round!" their dad, Lyle, joked then returned to making pancakes.

Meanwhile, the girls' mum—Alice—squirrelled away at the crossword, nibbling the end of her pencil. "Drat!" she exclaimed. "I've made a mistake!"

"You are a mistake," taunted Cecilia.

"Err, no! That's not a nice thing to say, missy. It might be your birthday but that's no way to talk to ya' mum."

Her dad came rushing at her, brandishing a greasy spoon. He held it up to Cecilia's chin, grinning from ear to ear.

"What have you done with my daughter?" he said playfully. "And when are you planning on bringing her back?"

"Never!" Cecilia hissed dramatically, squeezing her eyes into a villainous glare.

"Why, why, WHY!" Lyle broke down into a mock lamentation, dramatically falling to his knees and reaching his arms towards the sky, spoon falling to the floor, butter dripping everywhere.

"You're such a doofus, Dad," Cecilia chuckled through another sip of sweet tea.

"You're cleaning that up, by the way, Lyle," said Alice without looking up from her crossword.

"No, I'm not," said Lyle. "Tatty to the rescue!" Tatty was their cat and he hopped onto the floor quick as a flash at the mention of his name. Lyle retrieved the spoon and flung it into the sink, while Tatty licked the greasy patch of kitchen floor. Lyle flipped the last pancake and plonked it onto a pile he had already made.

"All right, all right, grub's up! Dig in, you scallies," said Lyle as he put the pile of steaming hot pancakes in the centre of the table. "Eat 'til your eyes are bulging out of your head! We've got a long day."

Ten minutes later, Cecilia was picking at the remains on her plate, breakfast now resting happily in her stomach, when she was distracted by Hester climbing up on her chair. Hester cleared her throat and wiped her sticky hands on her pyjamas and through a mouth smudged with raspberry jam was about to speak when Cecilia interrupted her.

"What are you doing?" she asked.

Hester, even at the tender age of eight, fancied herself as a bit of a scholar and found any occasion when people were gathered together as a chance to recite a poem or a speech she had "prepared earlier". She was going to write the speeches for a politician when she grew up. Hester unfolded a small piece of paper and began orating.

"We are gathered here today..."

"You pinched that, that's not your writing," heckled Cecilia.

Hester continued undeterred, "...to celebrate the birth and life of my dear sister, Cecilia Hudson-Gray, and I would like to personally mark the occasion with a gift and this wonderful speech I have written. Thank you." She sat back down. There was a light scattering of applause.

"That was a lovely gesture, Hester," said their mum, patting her on the back.

"So, Cecilia, do you think you deserve a present?" said Hester. Her eyes were bright and excited. "I hope you like it. If you don't, it won't go to waste—I can always keep it for myself."

She disappeared from the room for a moment and came back holding a crumpled brown paper bag that had been very badly taped shut. With a lot of Sellotape. Hester dumped her present on Cecilia's lap. "Here."

Cecilia could see how excited she was but knew that Hester had previous as far as presents were concerned: for Christmas she'd given her a broken alarm clock from the 1970s.

"Oh, it's heavier than it looks. Thanks, Hess."

When Cecilia finally managed to open the present, it was surprisingly marvellous. Hester had saved up her pocket money (that is, she used what was left of her pocket money after she had bought herself a new fountain pen) to buy a vintage marble from the old bric-a-brac store down the road from their granny. She had seen it one afternoon, when she and Granny had gone into the shop for a snoop. There was something magical about the way it caught the light, and Hester and Granny had decided that it was super special and that Cecilia simply had to have it for her birthday.

The marble was large, not quite as big a tennis ball but on the way there. It had an oily layer on its outer surface onto which a pattern of silvery white markings had been etched. When Cecilia held it up to the light, she could see through a chip on its surface into a misty white centre with a constellation of silvery sparkles. It had an enchanting way of reflecting the colours around it, catching the pink on Cecilia's pyjamas and the umber in Hester's eyes.

"Wow. Cool."

"Looks like the universe, doesn't it?" Hester said.

Cecilia stared at it. "Yeah. Thanks, Hess, it's gorgeous." Cecilia secretly thought that she was getting a bit old for toys but in this case she'd make an exception. It was more of a curiosity than a toy, plus it looked like it was made of glass and children aren't usually allowed to play with things made of glass. She was definitely old enough to look after something fragile.

"Let's have a look, missy," said her dad, holding out his hand. "Cor, that's a corker, that is, Hess, nice one." And they high-fived.

"I thought you could put it in this." Hester handed her sister a piece of gold string with a tangle of wires at the end.

"What is it?" asked Cecilia.

"It's a necklace, dummy. Look, it fits in here like this!" Hester demonstrated how to insert the marble into the contraption she had devised and handed it back to her sister, "Then you can wear it on special occasions!"

"Wow, Hess, that's really lovely and so creative," Cecilia said, trying to hide some of her discomfort. She had already guessed what was coming next and she didn't like the idea.

"Thanks. I knew you'd like it and the best part is: it's a special occasion today because it's your birthday, so you get to wear it all day!"

Cecilia winced a little. She really did love the marble but she wasn't sure she wanted to wear it. After all, it wasn't that cool. It sort of looked like something that had been pulled out of the rubbish, tangled up with all the string and wire, but she really didn't want to hurt Hester's feelings and it was only for one day and she could always tuck it under her jumper.

"Lucky me," she said drily with a wink and a cheesy smile. Hester was clearly ecstatic. Cecilia shot her dad a look that cried save me but he just shrugged in reply.

Cecilia unwrapped the presents from her mum and dad after that: a sketchbook, some watercolours and a brand-new junior microscope set.

"We know you love all that technology stuff: iPads, jPads, kPads and whatnot," joked her dad, "but we wanted to get you something a bit more hands on."

"Something that would inspire you," added her mum.

"Yeah, something that didn't need charging up," said her dad.

"I love it, guys, I absolutely love it. Thanks." Cecilia smiled.

"Right then, you lovely lot, let's get a groove on! There's a world out there waiting for us," said their mum. Once again there was thunder heard shaking through the floors of the house.

2

Roll with It

Hester was skipping ahead, humming to herself and picking bits off bushes and throwing the debris in the air like confetti. Cecilia, however, was trailing behind in a bit of a mood because they weren't allowed to bring any "technology" with them, which had meant she wasn't allowed her mobile. Her mum and dad were walking together talking about how rainbows are formed. When Cecilia overheard she picked up the pace—she loved science.

"Raindrops act like prisms and refract the light," said her mum, all matter of fact.

"Nonsense!" exclaimed her dad. "Raindrops are the tears

of clouds passing over the wonder, pain and beauty of the world. A prism is just a type of triangle. Come on now, Alice, you know better than that!"

Alice looked frustrated.

"Mum's right actually, Dad," said Cecilia, looping his arm.

He was really trying to wind her mum up now, smiling cheekily and nudging Cecilia in the ribs. "Rainbows are formed from the souls of lost shooting stars that have been pulled into Earth's atmosphere, where they mingle with these tears."

"Shut up, Lyle. You'll confuse Cecilia. We don't want her getting into her exams and writing poems when she's supposed to be answering questions about geography or science!"

Cecilia had always loved science. Where other people saw a blue sky she saw a curious world of questions that led to explanations. A hamburger wasn't just a hamburger, oh no. It was a stage in a life cycle, a food chain, a chemical reaction and a transfer of energy. It could all be broken down and retraced step by tiny step to the beginning of existence, and further still. Oh, don't get her wrong, she could still see the beauty in the world to which she belonged, but her awe came from how a thing came to be in the first place and where it would go next on its journey, not just what it looked like.

The family arrived at the Underground station, where a few members of station staff were milling around, chatting, smiling, pointing people in the right direction. Next to Cecilia in the ticket hall, standing there looking at a white board was an old man with a curly white afro. He was reading the quote of the day:

Some of the most beautiful things are born of mistakes
—ANON

Cecilia stared at it while the rest of her family faffed with Oyster cards and stubborn machines that will accept this and won't accept that.

"What does it mean?" Cecilia said absent-mindedly in a voice just shy of a whisper.

The old man wiped his nose with a tired hanky. "That occasionally beauty happens by accident. What do you think?" he said, tucking his hanky in his pocket and slowly buttoning up his coat. Cecilia noticed he had a button missing at the very top.

"Well, if that were the case, wouldn't that make just about everything beautiful?" Cecilia offered.

"It's a nice way to look at things, don't you think? Even the things that don't happen on purpose bring colour and vibrancy to this funny old world!" The man looked at Cecilia with a pair of dark eyes that had been made cloudy around the edges by the passing of time. Then he picked up his plastic bag and left. "Goodbye," he said sincerely.

Hester trotted over and started tugging at Cecilia's coat.

"Err, why were you talking to that dusty old man?"

"Argh! You're so rude, Hester. Imagine if you heard someone say that about Granny!"

"I was only asking," said Hester sheepishly, feeling burned and a bit confused. She tried to defend herself. "You can't help true facts, anyway, Cecilia, because he was old and I only wondered why you were talking to him. Simple as that."

Hester and Cecilia rejoined their parents and they floated down the escalator to the tunnels below.

They waited on the edge of the platform for their train to arrive, mumbles of conversation echoing around the tunnels. Cecilia tiptoed to the edge, her feet poised just over the yellow line, staring into the black hole of the tunnel as the two tiny bright eyes of the Tube train grew bigger and bigger. Suddenly she felt a weight around her neck, as though the marble necklace was pulling her over the edge, choking her. She was whipped back hastily by her dad seizing her by the shoulders.

"Cecilia, what on earth are you doing? You'll get your head knocked off!"

Cecilia wasn't quite sure what had happened. She hadn't even realised that she was in any sort of danger. But there in the headlights of the oncoming train, she had felt something stirring in the pit of her stomach and the weight of a world around her neck as she teetered on the edge. She shuddered and shook off a sinister feeling as she let out a deep breath.

"Please stand back behind the yellow line!" a monotone voice called as if mocking her from the loudspeaker.

"See," said Hester. "You silly sausage!"

They boarded the train and rode a few stops, then got off to change trains. The sound of a trumpet danced on the ceilings of the tunnels and into the open ears of passers-by. The family wriggled their way through the crowd but Cecilia stopped to see where the sound was coming from. The atmosphere melted into a blur of colours and background noise as she stood there entranced. She looked down at the busker's feet and where one would normally see a scattering of coins, there was a trumpet case bejewelled with gems and buttons. Cecilia was consumed by the music watching the busker's dreadlocks swaying as she gently rocked from side to side. Cecilia smiled and reached into her pocket.

"Cecilia!" shouted her dad, who was getting cross now, "Don't wander off like that! What has got into you all of a sudden?"

Cecilia broke out of her trance. "Sorry, Dad, it was just the music is really cool and the buttons... I was—"

"Yes, yes, come on, come on," her dad said hurriedly.

As they turned to leave, Cecilia felt in her pocket again for some change to give the busker, but by the time she had finished fishing around, discovering only a ten-pence piece and an open packet of Cherry Drops, the busker seemed to have upped and left—rather hastily, Cecilia thought.

"Hester," Cecilia called as she caught up with her sister. "I hope you don't mind but I'm going to take the necklace off for a bit. It's quite heavy and I'm not feeling so good."

"Oh, OK," said Hester. She looked a little bit upset. "I didn't think of that. I know, I'll make it into a ring when we get home instead!"

"Sure," said Cecilia, hoping she would forget.

Cecilia paused a moment and undid the knot of string around her neck, sighing with relief as it came off. But as she held the marble in her hand a passer-by knocked it out of her grasp. The marble came loose from its wire setting and fell to the floor; she watched it bounce heavily along the ground, heading back towards the platform they'd come from. Cecilia hurried after it, trying to catch it as she went. It bounced and landed with a thud back on the empty train that was still waiting on the platform. Speeding towards the carriage, she saw a flash of bright light as she jumped across the yellow line and landed on board. Seizing the marble in her hand, she shoved it in her coat pocket and turned back to leave, but as she did so the doors beeped and slid shut and in an instant she was swallowed whole. In the distance she could see her family rushing towards her through the smudged glass as the train snaked away into the tunnel ahead.

Cecilia became aware very quickly that she was the only passenger on board. She began to panic when the train failed to stop at any of the stations that it passed, some with names she had never heard of before. It travelled faster and faster, deeper and deeper—she could tell because her ears kept popping and she kept trying to yawn to release the pressure. All at once she was plunged into darkness. She had never experienced darkness like it, thick and heavy.

Frightening thoughts formed and danced into the black and became frenzied before: SNAP! The carriage lights flashed back on, flickering like blinking eyes. She sucked in her breath, feeling the train slow to a stop. Steadying herself, she watched as the train arrived at a station. The doors opened, an invitation for her to get off, but this was a station she definitely didn't recognise.

Cecilia stood frozen in the artificial lights of the train carriage for some time before even daring to breathe. She could see from the light being thrown out on the other side of the doors that there was a small platform covered in soot. She waited for something to happen. Nothing happened. There was only stillness, silence and the imperceptible passing of time. No clock ticked but she felt as though an eternity was passing through her with each beat of her heart. A dusty mouse scuffing through the soot brought her back to the moment. Was it wearing a pair of shoes and a jumper? Cecilia moved closer to look but it had already disappeared. Now at the mouth of the doors, she knew for the first time in her life the weight of being nowhere. She looked for signs: there were none. She called for a response: none came. After what felt like hours of waiting and shouting for help, her fear abandoned her briefly and she stepped off the train. No sooner had she left the train did the doors clap shut and the train leave her.

Cecilia found herself abandoned in a false night, the light from the train dimming as it departed. Her body shook and the sound of her own whimpering was as close as if she were listening to it on headphones. Her breathing hastened and she burst into tears. Cecilia's legs wobbled and gave way: she crumpled to the ground where she wept violently, terrified and helpless against the colossal depth of the darkness all around her.

3

The End of the Line

A thought of Hester popped into Cecilia's head and gave her a moment of calm. In the safety of her mind she remembered all the times they had played hide and seek in the dark corners of their family home. Oh, how she wanted to go home. A longing grew in her chest, but she tried to hold it back, swallow the lump in her throat. Deep down Cecilia knew that in her current situation if she thought too long about getting home, the fear that she might never return could become real and suffocate her entirely. So she imagined that Hester was just hiding in the dark and all she had to do was find her; she felt better, stronger even, like she wasn't alone any more because this was all a game, and eventually Hester would jump out at her and they would laugh. Then they could steal the raw jelly from the top cupboard, like they had so many times before, and eat it in the middle of the night.

But this was not a game of hide and seek. In the end Cecilia had no choice but to get moving. It couldn't possibly get any worse. She realised that the only person who could make a difference to her situation was herself. The train had gone, taking its light with it. Her eyes widened as they tried to find something to focus on, searching for some direction in the endless black. She shuffled forwards and found a wall; it was a huge comfort to feel something solid against her hands. The tunnel only ran in two directions as far as she should tell: left and right. This was useful because it meant she only had to make a decision based on two options. She squinted hard and coming into focus on the right there seemed to be the hint of a colour, an aura of orangey-brown. To the left there was nothing but black. Really she had no choice but to head towards the light. Cecilia took a deep breath and began to feel her way along the wall.

She imagined what it might be like to go deep-sea diving at night, never quite sure what strange or fantastic creature might jump out at you. The thought was terrifying. Once again she remembered it was a bad idea to think too much. For a time she hummed the tune to 'Greensleeves' that she had learnt on the recorder at school, but her throat soon felt sore and dry. She moved faster towards the source of the light, and as she drew nearer she could just about make out an archway with autumnal colours shining through. Was she imagining it? She paused a moment, afraid to let go of the wall. She almost turned to look back at how far she had come but changed her mind. Wiping her hands on her coat, she stepped into the light.

Her skin prickled. It was actually warm, which pleased her as she realised how cold she had been. Before walking through the archway, she noticed some writing, covered in dirt and gunge. She wiped it off with the corner of her jacket and whispered the words to herself:

> *"Those who wander will regret*
> *If they return they will forget*
> *For those who step outside the lines*
> *Will lose all sense of place and time."*

Cecilia considered it a moment before walking through into the small atrium in front of her. It was quite beautiful. The walls were pockmarked and there were tiny fragments of broken mirror glittering about the place that picked up the gentle hue of orange and shone it back. The orange light came from fluorescent tubes that ran round the edges of the space and climbed the walls, creating a pattern on the ceiling like the underside of an umbrella. It reminded Cecilia of a funfair—but without any people or music or candy floss or rides. So, really, on second thought it wasn't like a funfair at all—and she certainly wasn't having much fun!

There, directly in front of her, was a window. It looked like an old ticket office but there seemed to be nothing beyond the glass. Next to the window was a door. It was a large metal door, and on it painted in capital letters the word ATTENDANT was peeling off.

Cecilia nervously approached the window. She felt the same as when she had taken the long walk from her seat to the stage to do a reading in assembly. It was the worst. Her fingertips tingled with anticipation as she reached out and tapped the glass. Cecilia peered in but there was no response. She walked over to the door and tapped politely underneath the writing. She waited and waited.

"This is silly," she said aloud and made a fist and banged heavily on the metal. No sooner had she banged than she was answered: three loud bangs hammered back. She was held stiff in a moment of terror. Cecilia banged again; after all, what choice did she have? The same bang was returned. She changed the rhythm; the new rhythm was repeated and then out of nowhere she lost her temper and shouted, "Are you going to open this door or what?"

It was extremely rude but Cecilia was desperate and she had no idea what was happening to her or where she was. All she could do was hope that there wasn't something awful behind the door. She bit her lip as she waited for something to happen. Cecilia jammed her hands in her pockets. What if the person behind the door was dangerous—what were they doing all the way down here in the first place? The door swung open and a loud, deep, musical voice bellowed down from above.

"What are you doing here, little thing?"

Cecilia stood there, astonished. The man in front of her was not just a man: he was also an animal and he appeared to have the face of a fox. It's rude to stare, thought Cecilia. This can't be happening, thought Cecilia. Act normal, thought Cecilia.

"Hello," she said. "I'm lost!" She laughed nervously.

"That you are." His accent had a hint of Scottish in it. For some reason this put Cecilia at ease, perhaps it was because it meant that at the very least she was still on her own planet.

"I realised I was lost a while ago and I've been wandering about for hours!" She looked at his face curiously. Maybe he's getting ready for a fancy dress party, she thought, or perhaps she'd stumbled onto a secret location where they were shooting a film—but he sure looked real.

"And what, pray tell, do you want me to do about your loss, little thing?"

"Well, I was hoping that you might point me in the right direction?"

The fox-faced man was strikingly handsome and quite tall—at least as tall as her dad, who was six-foot-two. He had spiky black whiskers and dazzling amber eyes, and although she could see he had a set of sharp teeth, they didn't seem scary—rather, mischief whispered around the corners of his mouth as though he was about to share a secret.

"Oh dear," he said, folding his arms and shaking his head. "It's a very, very long time since I had a wanderer in my midst. I think you'd better come in and sit down. Don't worry, we will bring you up to speed, help you fill in the gaps! In the end, you know, there is no 'right' direction." He smiled. "My name is Kuffi, by the way. Now, don't you think it's rather rude of you to disturb someone at his work with all that banging and huffing and puffing and not even introduce yourself?"

"I'm really sorry," Cecilia replied, holding out her hand. "I'm Cecilia Hudson-Gray."

"No thanks, I'd rather not if you don't mind. You're filthy! Pleased to meet you, nonetheless," he said, patting her on the head with a fury palm. She might have expected Kuffi to have paws but his hands were the same shape as a human hand, just covered in the same fur that covered the rest of him—thick, silky red fox fur.

"Oh. Pleased to meet you too, Kuffi!" Cecilia said, looking down at her own soot-stained hands. They were so black it was as though she had been touching the souls of shadows and she wondered what the rest of her must look like!

It was dark inside Kuffi's cabin. However, Cecilia had begun to notice that there were different types of darkness. It seemed there were different shades that made a person or thing feel or look a certain way. In Kuffi's room it was like a warm tropical evening in late summer, and although the room was quite sparse (aside from heaps of books), it felt cosy. The light was low and comforting and the entire room, which wasn't very big, smelled sweetly of ginger and fresh earth. Cecilia thought the piles of books scattered everywhere looked like discarded empty crisp packets and her stomach rumbled as she thought of crisps. It seemed like such a long time since breakfast—then she remembered she had that half a packet of Cherry Drops in her pocket. She got them out and began unwrapping the crumpled tube eagerly. She held out the packet to Kuffi first, of course.

"Cherry Drop?" asked Cecilia, warily holding out the packet.

"Was that you making that noise then? Why were you growling at me?" he asked.

"I'm not, honestly, it was just my stomach rumbling. I'm a bit hungry, that's all."

"It sounds monstrous."

"It does feel like there's a monster in there, to be honest," said Cecilia, crossing her arms across her tummy.

"Goodness! How awful. It sounds rather vicious. You scared me there a moment!"

"You scared me too!"

Cecilia and Kuffi chuckled with one another briefly, breaking the tension.

"Sit down, sit down. I'll fix you some tea but I'm afraid I have nothing to eat here. It's best not to keep food on the premises. It attracts rat-faces, the pesky little thieves."

"Oh dear," she mumbled, hoping that the rat-face people wouldn't be as big as Kuffi—that would be terrifying. Kuffi went over to a kitchenette at the back of the room where there was a pan on a small hob over a bowl of coals. Cecilia sat down, popping a Cherry Drop in her mouth, then stuffing the packet back in her pocket. She left another one on a small hexagonal table. "I'll leave this here for you for later if you like," she said.

"No open flames, you will remember that rule, right?" he asked, poking at the glowing embers.

"Sure." Cecilia shrugged.

Kuffi got a set of keys out of his pocket and unlocked the cupboard below a basin near the hot coals. He brought out a large green glass bottle, which he uncorked and measured out the exact amount of water he wanted into a small blue china teacup, then added two more dashes to the pan before putting the bottle away and locking the cupboard. Cecilia found the whole process very serious. Kuffi stared into the liquid as he stirred the concoction, the steam rising up to tickle his whiskers. He added what looked like some spices, and something resembling a root of ginger, but no tea bag as such.

When it was ready he brought it over to Cecilia and put it down very carefully next to the Cherry Drop on the hexagonal table between two armchairs, one of which Cecilia was sitting in.

"Thank you, Kuffi. Aren't you going to have any?"

"Oh no, you go for it. I'll have mine tomorrow," he said, matter of fact.

"Tomorrow?" Cecilia thought this was a very strange response.

"Yes, tomorrow. Water is in short supply, so drink up!" he commanded.

Cecilia sipped the drink quietly; it was soothing, hot and spicy, tasting just like the smells in the warm room, it was quite rejuvenating.

*　*　*

The two of them sat there a while, chatting. Kuffi had a way of making her feel very much at ease. Cecilia was so desperate to escape her situation and go home, she found it hard to believe that the creature in front of her had a fox face. Between the gaps in their conversation she had a second when she feared that he might try and eat her, but nothing about him seemed to suggest that this was his intention. In fact, he seemed pleased of her company. Somehow, in the midst of what was an awful set of circumstances, she even found herself laughing at a few of his jokes. She realised that normally Kuffi would seem frightening but there was nothing normal about what was happening. So she was grateful for the distraction and, as it turned out, Kuffi was fascinating. As Cecilia blew on her tea to cool it down, he asked her a really important question that confirmed he meant her no harm.

"Cecilia. Are you OK?" He said this very gently and Cecilia winced a little bit.

"I'm OK, I think. A bit confused but it's nice to be somewhere. It was very dark and lonely out there for a bit."

"The Black of Beyond is no place for anyone, let alone a little thing like you."

"The Black of Beyond?" she asked, feeling a little confused.

"The Black of Beyond is the place where you were lost. Legend has it that if you just keep walking you can end up walking from somewhere to nowhere. You're a 'Wanderer'— that is what we call fellows like yourself: confused inhabitants, ordinary dwellers, that have 'wandered off' and been lost in the Black of Beyond. When fellows like yourself turn up here, they've been gone so long or been so far into the Black of Beyond that they lose a sense of what's real. It's like their memories have been completely wiped. Most of the time they have the most magical stories to tell, though."

"Oh, well, it felt like for ever but I am sure it can't have been more than an hour or two," she said confidently. "I just really want to get home."

"And do you know where that is?" Kuffi seemed to be asking a lot of questions.

"Well, back the way I came, I guess, back to the train that brought me here, to my family and my house and my cat. They will be worried about me by now, I'm sure."

"Cecilia, there are some souls that get lost in the dark of the tunnels and then lost in their minds; their imaginations take over. They even come to believe there is some sort of other world above us, dazzled by light and full of abundance. We all dream of a better place from time to time but these poor souls have become disillusioned by the darkness; they seem to have forgotten the dwellers and the society they belong to and they go in search of some light at the end of the tunnel. The Black of Beyond is a scary place but that's all it is—the dark place at the end of the line. Maybe you are one of these poor fellows and you've forgotten your place or where you belong? Wanderers often look like you. Jasper, he's similar, sort of bald... perhaps all your fur has fallen out and your whiskers... Where are they?" Kuffi said, inspecting her.

"What, no! I've never had any fur or whiskers." She almost laughed at how ridiculous it sounded.

"Well, you still have quite a mane on top of your head," Kuffi said, pointing at her crown of curls. "I know, why don't we take a walk and reintroduce you to the dwellers? You can have a nap first if you like and then we will see if we can't jog your memory a bit, remind you of the society that you belonged to before you went walking about in the dark."

"I'm not sure you understand," Cecilia said. She still felt compelled to try to convince him one more time in case he'd misunderstood. "I can't tell you where I am now but before I ended up here, I was on a train and before that I was walking down the road with my family. There was a sky above my head and the sun kept popping out from behind the clouds. The birds were singing in the trees and it was a lovely day out we had planned for my birthday."

"Sun, what's a sun?" Kuffi said to Cecilia plainly.

How can anyone live without sunlight, she thought.

"You're joking, right?" Cecilia asked.

"Of course not," he said, settling into his seat to listen to her.

"OK. Well... it's a big ball of gas burning really, really far away from this planet—Earth. It helps things to grow and live, it keeps us warm and helps us know when to be awake and when to sleep," she said, willing him to give in and say it was all a big joke, a birthday prank like on those TV shows that trick people for everyone else's entertainment.

"I see." Kuffi seemed to be taking it in as a frown crept across his brow and his whiskers twitched involuntarily.

"Cecilia, that's a marvellous story. The sun, what a fantastic imagination you have!" And just like that, he smiled and pushed aside what she was saying.

Cecilia was so frustrated. Why didn't he believe her? She was about to burst as she stood up from the armchair. "You have to believe me, Kuffi. I'm from up there, from outside!" She pointed up towards the crumbly ceiling.

But the more Cecilia tried to convince Kuffi of the outside world, the more fantastical and ridiculous her words began to sound. She got carried away, trying to explain her lush green world with its rolling oceans and snow-capped mountains, gesticulating and describing things in detail, and with each word she saw his pity grow through the expression on his face. She slowed down as it began to sound more and more like a fantasy world she had conjured up.

They shared a moment of silence before Kuffi said kindly, "It sounds beautiful, Cecilia. I'm not sure what happens out in the Black of Beyond but the few fellows that do return to the tunnels—all, I'm sorry to say, have similar stories. It's nothing to be ashamed of, though."

Cecilia went to sit back down and found she was sitting uncomfortably on the marble Hester had given her. She got up and took it out of her pocket.

"What's that you have there?" said Kuffi curiously.

"It's just a marble, a birthday present from my sister, Hester..." she said, her words tailing off.

"What is a marble?"

"This," said Cecilia, thrusting the object towards him.

"Me, oh, my," Kuffi exclaimed. "Well, I never. A marble, you say? You are lucky to have been gifted such a thing." His eyes were bright and fiery.

As Cecilia plopped it back in her pocket, Kuffi stood up. He seemed excited and smiled widely, smoothing out his rather snug-fitting navy suit and smart pillbox hat, he walked over to the kitchenette, picked something up and returned to where Cecilia was sitting. He held out a sharp, shard-like piece of broken mirror that gleamed as it caught the light.

"I'm sorry to have to do this to you, Cecilia," he said gravely, brandishing it like a knife.

4

To Market, to Market

Kuffi moved closer to Cecilia, flashing the slice of broken mirror. She looked up at him, terror stricken. He recognised the picture of fear on her face, looked at the shard he was holding and stopped himself. "Oh dear," he chuckled. "It's OK," he said reassuringly. "I would never hurt you, it's just very rare to see someone walking around with buttons used as adornments or fastenings. I don't know where you got that coat but we need to remove the buttons; you can't walk around with all that wealth stuck to you now, can you?" Kuffi held out his hand for the coat and Cecilia took it off and gave it to him.

Cecilia watched as Kuffi went to work. The coat had several buttons down the left hand side—six, to be precise—and two smaller ones on either side on the top pockets. Kuffi explained that only those held in high esteem adorned themselves with buttons; he personally thought it was quite vulgar. Buttons were best used in exchange for goods at Market Square. Kuffi's own clothes—he demonstrated by adjusting his top collars—were fastened with little hooks. "Clever, huh?" he said, tidying his green polka-dot cravat. Cecilia knew it was a cravat because her grandpa had worn one, and he had explained that it was neither a scarf nor a tie but something in between.

Kuffi collected the buttons together and handed them to Cecilia. "You're going to need these to feed the monster in your stomach," he joked. "Come on then, enough idle chat. Let's go and get something to eat!"

Kuffi checked all the doors and switched on a red neon sign in the window, which read OUT, and they exited the room through a back door.

The two walked for some time along a dimly lit narrow passage. The ceiling was low and seemed to be made of compacted dirt. They came to an opening and it became quite bright. The space before them was flooded with orange light thrown out from a criss-cross of fluorescent tubes overhead. At the centre of the clearing there was a vehicle on two parallel tracks pointing towards an opening. The vehicle was similar to a dune buggy but had bicycle wheels with no rubber on the tyres. It had a small engine in the undercarriage and motorbike handlebars. Kuffi was clearly very proud of this piece of equipment. He walked around it, examining it and polishing up the badge.

"What is it?" asked Cecilia.

"What is it!" Kuffi exclaimed. "Only the best track rider you can get. What is it, indeed!" Kuffi scoffed, clearly offended.

Cecilia was beginning to feel a little bit exasperated but instead of showing it, she had an idea and decided to join in. After all, there was no point fighting her circumstances; she needed all the help she could get and Kuffi had a wealth of knowledge to share.

"I meant... What a beaut! Woweeee, soooo shiny and all!" Cecilia could see that Kuffi was flattered.

"She sure is," Kuffi said with a swagger in his step as he polished the handlebars with his furry hand. "Top of the range: Wasp 75, best model to date. Bet you haven't seen one like this before?"

Cecilia looked at it; the shape of the handlebars and the headlights, made it look a bit like a wasp.

"Erm, no," said Cecilia, smiling to herself—it wasn't as if she were lying. If this was top of the range, then imagine what Kuffi would think of the cars, trucks, boats and planes where she came from.

Kuffi flung her a helmet. "Catch!" he shouted. Cecilia laughed as she whipped the helmet out of the air. "Nice one," remarked Kuffi as Cecilia put her helmet on.

"Be my guest!" Kuffi said as he helped her up onto the Wasp 75. He climbed on in front of her and pulled a cord much like the light switch in her bathroom at home and the

Wasp 75's engine began to gurgle. Kuffi twisted the grips on the handlebars and revved the engine, which let out little bursts of roaring sound. "Hold on tight," he shouted above the noise and Cecilia grabbed his waist, and with that they zipped off down the line.

It was thrilling riding through the tunnels. Almost immediately the pokiness of the tunnels transformed into lofty caverns in an array of colours and sizes. For a while Cecilia was absorbed in the moment, utterly forgetting the distress of how she had ended up down here in the first place. There was so much to see along the way. There were tunnel dwellers who lived in a kind of collective hive: hollows had been dug into the surface of the walls, one on top of the other, and there were various ladders and pulley systems constructed to help those who didn't have the gift of flight to get to the higher levels. The dwellers themselves were creatures unlike any Cecilia had ever seen. They were different shapes and species, composite beings of various creatures she recognised from living above ground but human-sized: mice, rabbits, frogs, and there were birds too, lots of birds. All of the dwellers had human attributes, but they didn't have skin—their arms and legs and torsos were covered in fur and feathers, hair and scales. It was a bit unsettling at first. Cecilia felt the dwellers might be wearing masks or costumes. However, up close you could see that that was how they were made. There were dwellers dotted all about the place, high and low, leaning out of windows and doorways. It was so strange but also strangely familiar. There, underground, these creatures were going about their daily business, chatting, hanging out with one another, playing games and living a seemingly ordinary existence. It was a comfort to see them getting on in such a way and reminded her of back home. But she'd never wanted to sit on the doorstep with Benny Frinks, the boy who lived next door to her, more than she did now. Cecilia saw a pug-face and a sparrow-face playing a game of chess. The sparrow-man was even smoking a pipe, or at least that's what it looked like—the smoke was pink—but they were speeding by too fast for a second look.

At last Kuffi and Cecilia pulled into a parking lot with loads of other track riders. Kuffi pointed out some of the other models as they looked for a parking spot. From there it didn't take long to walk to Market Square and by now Cecilia was ravenous.

"Here we are, little thing," said Kuffi as they passed through an elaborately carved gateway. "Let's get some grub and you never know—maybe seeing the hustle and bustle of Market Square will jog your memory a little bit too." He pointed to the square that contained the underground market below them. "Voila!"

"Whoa! Kuffi, it's MASSIVE!" Cecilia and Kuffi stood at the top of some limestone steps overlooking the market. It was a sight to behold. Hundreds of citizens—dwellers—working at the stalls and carts below them: bellowing, whistling, cooing, grunting, shoving and pushing to get the best deals and peddle their wares.

"Remember this place now? Pretty hard to forget, hey?" Kuffi said hopefully, as if he were trying to convince her.

Cecilia didn't remember it, of course, because she had never in her life seen anywhere like it before—but she lied because after all what was the point in arguing? Anyway, in such a strange place, it was better to have a friend who could show her the way; she daren't scare Kuffi off because she liked him. He made her feel safe and she wanted him to like her back so she pretended. It was best for both their sakes.

"Kuffi, there is something coming back to me." She pointed to the most obvious feature at the end of Market Square: a long platform, lit up with tiny lantern lights above and below. There, in the middle, was a podium and a large banner acting as a backdrop with a handsome golden bird-like man featured on it. Corvus Community–Carpe Noctem was embroidered beautifully underneath him.

"How could I ever forget that guy?" said Cecilia.

Kuffi bowed his head a little. "Yes. You're quite right, hard to forget him. Jacques d'Or and his community of ever-present guards. Carpe noctem: Seize the night! You'd think that lot had invented the dark, the way they harp on about it." Kuffi had forgotten himself and became aware that he was in public. "I beg my pardon, what am I saying?" He corrected himself, clearly uncomfortable. Kuffi heaved a sigh, which seemed to hang there a moment, and once again his whiskers twitched as though they had a life of their own. Kuffi tried to lift the mood. "Let's go get some grub!"

The two descended the steps and entered the fray. It was a bit like being on holiday, going to a new city and everything seeming a little bit strange, then an hour or so later you've adjusted and feel quite at home. In the end, most folk are pretty similar, Cecilia thought, even if they look a bit different or speak a different language. "Everybody's got to eat," as her granny said.

Kuffi stopped at a stall with the word GRUB painted in fluorescent green, rather untidily, on a piece of rotting old wood. A woodlouse popped out and scuttled across the letter G. It was pretty busy but somehow Cecilia and Kuffi pushed their way to the front of the queue. Cecilia felt a bit embarrassed about this—she'd never been one to push, although Hester often got away with it.

"All right, Robbie!" called Kuffi.

"Koof, matey, you up for some lovely grub?" Robbie chirruped happily.

Robbie couldn't have been more beautiful; he was a robin-face, a chap of miniature proportions, probably about as big as Hester, with a sweet voice and jovial disposition, and despite his size he made a lot of noise. He flitted about the cart to and fro passing small wooden bowls of grub to the folk below, in exchange for buttons.

"The usual?" he twittered, his red breast bursting through the top of his shirt like a hairy chest.

"Times two." Kuffi gestured to Cecilia.

"What 'ave we got 'ere then, Koof?" he whistled, managing to stay still for a split second.

"This is my new friend, Cecilia." He leant over the counter and whispered into Robbie's ear.

"Oh, right," Robbie twittered knowingly. "We'll soon

43

set you right, lovely." He handed Kuffi two wooden bowls and Kuffi gave him a big blue button. "Keep the change!"

"Thanks, Koof. See you tomorrow!" And with that he darted off to serve the next customer.

Kuffi carried the bowls over to some benches where the two smushed themselves in next to the other occupants, sitting opposite each other. Kuffi got stuck in straight away but Cecilia looked down into her bowl cautiously. At first it looked like mushed-up rice, but on closer inspection she could see that there was something else mashed in with it. She dug around in the mush with a little wooden spoon, genuinely repulsed.

"What's wrong?" asked Kuffi through a mouthful.

"What is it, Kuffi?"

"It's grub, Cecilia," he said, chomping away hungrily.

"Yes. But what is grub?"

"Potatoes, onion, mushroom, a sprinkle of dirt and... earthworms," he replied, merrily shovelling another spoonful into his mouth.

Cecilia gulped. "Earthworms. Right, sure. I don't have to eat them though, Kuffi?"

"Why, yes, of course. They're fresh! That's when they're at their most nutritious, you silly potato face!"

"I'm not sure I like to eat earthworms, Kuffi." Cecilia was trembling. She tried to hide it by tucking her hands into her sleeves.

"What's not to like?" he asked.

Cecilia was a rational kind of person with a scientific mind; she knew this wouldn't kill her. Anyway, she thought,

I like trying new things... but eating worms? She frowned. All sorts of questions came flooding to mind.

"Are they definitely dead, Kuffi?" she asked. She couldn't stand the thought of them wiggling about in her mouth.

"Yes, Cecilia. Now eat up or that monster might get the better of you. Besides someone else will have it if you don't hurry up!"

Cecilia paused, looking into her bowl.

"Look, it's the cycle of life," Kuffi went on. "You eat that up quickly now and it will become part of you, keep you going and that kind of thing. Then it will come out of the other end and it will get eaten by—guess what? More earthworms. Full circle. We are all energy transferred, just in various forms! What you consume becomes a part of you, at least for a while. Surely it would be far worse now that this food has been made and put before you, not to eat it and let the earthworms and let their lives be wasted? They've no where left to go but your belly."

"OK, that's true," she said, nodding. "Eventually they'll go back to the ground and nourish it for other earthworms."

"Exactly. Try it. If you don't like it I will eat it," he said, licking his chops. "Look, they're delicious." Kuffi slurped up a worm like spaghetti. "Scrum-diddly-yum! You'll see and then you'll wonder why you were ever worried about eating this lovely grub!"

"OK," Cecilia whimpered. She lifted a spoonful to her mouth. Birds eat worms, she thought, and they're just fine. Besides, what's the difference between eating this and some chicken. It was all over very quickly and although she did not like the texture of worms in her mouth, the dish tasted mostly of potatoes and onions—and in the end she finished the lot. Cecilia looked down into her empty bowl and wondered if she'd ever go back to where she came from and if she did, whether Hester would believe she'd eaten worms to survive! Hester would probably love it and come up with some silly name for her, like "worm worshipper" or "wiggly-worm eater". She chuckled to herself as Kuffi collected the bowls.

"There you go," he said. "I know it's hard. Things might seem a little bit strange at the moment but it will get better. It's just, well, we want you to fit in, don't we?" It was almost as though Kuffi was trying to tell her something. "To be honest, we are all alone, wandering through the dark at various points in our lives." With that, Kuffi got up out of his seat.

Cecilia watched him walk over and chat to Robbie. Things seemed to have calmed down quite a bit at the grub stand now and the two of them were laughing and joking together. She watched a while and considered that things could be worse. At least she had made a friend.

5

Ducking and Diving

As Cecilia sat there digesting a stomach full of worms, she noticed a young lad in a hood, with a pair of antlers jutting out of two holes ripped in the top. She watched him carefully and realised he was watching her too. He beckoned her to come over to him with a motion of his head, but she quickly turned away, shoving her hands in her pockets and pretending to be preoccupied to avoid looking at him.

"What are you looking for in there, then?" came a youthful voice from behind her. It seemed she had company. Cecilia turned and found herself staring up at the stag-faced boy, the very creature she'd been trying to avoid. He had come to her.

"Sorry?" she said, acting dumb.

"Don't be. What have you got in there? I know, let's play a game. Whatever it is you've got in your pocket, I'll buy it off you!" he said, looking at her with black eyes that shone like tarnished silver.

"But you don't know what it is. What if it's just a piece of rubbish?" Cecilia replied, baffled.

"What's life without a little bit of a gamble, a little bit of risk? You just have to believe you're lucky and it usually works out!" he said confidently.

Cecilia sat there listening to him talk boisterously, feeling quite intimidated.

"Whatever it is, I'll buy it. Come on! Two buttons?"

"I haven't got anything," she lied.

"Ooohweeee, would you look at that?" said the stag-faced boy, pointing at the lights above. Cecilia brought her hands up to shield her eyes from the lights as she stared high into the hollows of the Market roof.

"Oldest trick in the book," he said, whipping the marble out of her pocket. He cupped it in both hands and brought it up to his eye. He peered into it. His jaw became slack and Cecilia watched him mouth the words "gee whiz". He was so distracted she managed to grab it back out of his hand.

"That's mine. Thief!" she said, just shy of shouting.

"Takes one to know one," he said childishly.

Just as the words left his mouth, Cecilia found Kuffi at her side.

"So, I see you've met Luke. Right rascal, this one, quick and witty." Kuffi pointed at his head. "My, your antlers have grown, Luke." Kuffi laughed. "He's harmless really, Cecilia." Kuffi laughed again, trying to embarrass the poor young buck.

"Sorry, Koof, I didn't know she was with you." He reminded her of any other surly teenage boy, like the boys that hung out in her local park getting into all sorts of mischief, but in Kuffi's presence he seemed humbled.

"Well, now you do. Off you go, son, and say hello to Jasper for me. Let him know we'll be popping in on him later, will you?"

"All right, Koof!" he said, shooting Cecilia a look that said: this isn't over yet! Cecilia got the distinct feeling he was right. It seemed that everyone knew Kuffi and everyone liked him; Cecilia was beginning to feel rather special walking around with him.

Cecilia was feeling much more herself and having Kuffi stick up for her had made her feel somewhat safer than she had before. Many of the market traders were beginning to pack up and just as she was beginning to grow tired, Kuffi smiled widely and pointed out a bookstall.

There were books piled high. Some even had familiar titles and authors. Cecilia found a handwritten leather-bound book called *The Diary of a Button Collector* sticking out of the bottom of one of the stacks. She shuffled it out like the bottom piece in a game of pick-up sticks, trying not to disturb the pile above.

"How do I buy this?" Cecilia asked Kuffi, interrupting the conversation he was having with a fox-face called Edwina. She had a sharp smile, smooth voice and teeth that looked like they could do serious damage. She also had beautiful shoulder-length red hair that matched her fur.

"It's worth a button, babe," Edwina answered, two dimples carving out her smile.

"Unless you have something else to exchange for it? I'm always on the look out for new curiosities and you don't look like you're from round here—got anything of interest for me?" She smiled at Kuffi, clearly flirting with him.

"Huh?" Cecilia was trying to read into what she was saying.

"You need to exchange something for it. Buttons are the best way to go. I'd hold on to that 'present' you were given, if I were you. You never know when you might need it," said Kuffi, helping her out.

"OK," said Cecilia, handing over one of the buttons that Kuffi had removed from her coat.

"Do you want me to look after it for you, Cecilia? We can have a read later when we get back."

"Cheers, Kuffi," said Cecilia as she passed it to him.

"*The Diary of a Button Collector*," he read aloud. "Thrilling, I bet!" He put it safely in his inside pocket.

At that moment something familiar caught Cecilia's eye. "*Great Expectations*, by Charles Dickens?" Cecilia was bursting with excitement "See, Kuffi, that guy, Charles Dickens, he's from where I come from, up there—the light at the end of the tunnel or whatever you call it!" She bellowed as she pointed to a book a little way above her head.

"No, he's not. Charles Dickens lives just off the lime line in the lime-light district with the other celebrated dwellers."

"Dickens is DEAD!" shouted Cecilia loudly, losing control of herself.

A hush came over the market. A murmur began, whispers spreading through the crowd before an old squirrel-face lady began wailing, "NO! Dickens is dead! DICKENS IS DEAD!"

Chaos broke out; people began rushing about in a huge commotion, spreading the news to one another. But it didn't last long. Overhead, circling in like ghosts of darkness, a group of cloaked bird-faces began to descend on the crowd. Fear settled in all around like a storm approaching and the chatter dimmed to whispers and then silence. Everything became very, very still. Swooping down and landing at different spots in the crowd, the black-winged birds took their positions to survey the dwellers. There were seven figures that inched their way through the dirt; they had the faces of jackdaws. The woman in charge was larger: a raven-face. She hopped up from the ground and flew into the air before gliding down onto the stage and walking up to the podium. Kuffi grabbed Cecilia's hand and looked at her very seriously, bringing a finger up to his snout with his spare hand that said suggested she didn't speak. No one spoke. In fact, they barely breathed. A spotlight flicked on and the hiss of speakers sent a sharp sound into the ears of the onlookers, forcing them to listen.

"Ladies and gentlefolk. Please compose yourselves," said the raven-face. The other birds strutted onto the stage one by one, a show of shadows with sharp black beaks and suits to match.

"What is all the fuss about?" the raven-face speaker said, moving in jolting twitches. A brave woman among the crowd in a deep red velvet coat, with a mouse-face, tentatively raised her hand, addressing the raven-face by name:

"Madame Helen, miss, we have just heard the news that Dickens is dead!" She wept.

"Nonsense. Who told you that?" Madame Helen asked.

There was silence once again and it was full of worried faces searching for someone to blame. Kuffi bent low and whispered in Cecilia's ear. "It's time to go, little thing. Do you remember where the Wasp 75 is?"

Cecilia nodded.

"Make your way though the crowd and meet me there. Do not stop and do not look back until you get there. Don't be scared and move very slowly. OK?"

Cecilia nodded again and began to move. It was terrifying. She tried not to bump anyone and she did pretty well at not being noticed. But she feared for Kuffi: he was big and tall.

She climbed the limestone steps until she reached the top where she followed the path back to the parking lot. It wasn't far and as she came up to it she could see the Wasp 75 right away. Cecilia broke into a run and went and hid behind the vehicle, grasping it tightly and trembling terribly. She felt awful, it was all her fault that trouble had broken out. If only she'd kept her mouth shut, she thought. Kuffi seemed to take such a long time but eventually she saw him enter the parking lot. He must've stayed back so as not to attract too much attention. Kuffi came over to the Wasp 75 and in a loud whisper he said, "I'm being followed, stay down."

Two of the guys Cecilia had just seen land in the crowd a few minutes before, the ones with jackdaw faces and black suits, swooped in on Kuffi. One landed right on top of the handlebars of the Wasp 75.

"What have we got here then, Julius?" said the smaller of the two bird-faced figures.

"Let's see, shall we, Marvin? Tall, ginger, pointy ears and a silly hat!" said Julius, knocking Kuffi's pillbox hat off his head.

"Sounds like Kuffi to me, Julius!" said Marvin. He sounded like such a telltale.

"Kuffi, Kuffi, Kuffi," tutted Julius and he kicked Kuffi's hat aside.

Marvin bounced up and down on the handlebars as Julius squared up to Kuffi. Julius sneered at Kuffi.

"ID papers, Mr Kuffi," he demanded, throwing his wings back and extending an arm from beneath.

Kuffi reached into his top pocket and handed over the papers.

"Mr Kuffi McAllister, are you aware that your ID papers are almost out of date? You better get that sorted, or next time we meet I'll be taking you in. Do you understand?" Julius began preening his jet-black feathers and flicked off a piece of fluff that had become caught. Kuffi stood proudly and quietly, looking quite unafraid. Cecilia stayed low; she felt so helpless as she listened to them trying to intimidate Kuffi.

"Cat got your tongue, Kuffi? That's not like you. Well, listen here, you're not so special that you don't have to pay to update your ID papers just like everybody else. There's, nothing more I'd like than to take you to Jacques d'Or!" drawled Julius from his humble spot as Kuffi towered over him. But he was far from being humble—he was a nasty piece of work, Cecilia could tell. "We will get you one day, you useless lump." Julius eyed up the Wasp 75.

"Nice set of wheels you got here. See this, Marvin?" Julius said, grabbing hold of the other end of the handlebars where Marvin was perched. As he walked round he kicked dirt in Cecilia's face. She tried not to breathe it in.

"It's only a matter of time before we take her for a spin." Julius' voice was dripping with contempt.

"Joyride, more like!" cackled Marvin, hopping swiftly into the air.

The two Corvus Community members made to leave, Julius kicking Kuffi's hat along in the dirt some way before leaping into the air, his parting words echoing through the tunnels.

"Watch your back, Kuffi. We'll be hiding in the shadows, waiting. Your time will come!"

Kuffi was very quiet. He walked over to his hat without saying a word and bent down to pick it up. On his way back to the Wasp 75, he dusted it off and tried to batter some shape back into it.

"Poor hat," he said when he had returned. "It sure has taken a beating." He placed it back on his head, completely disregarding what had just happened.

"Right then," he said. "We should get out of here. There's a bad smell about the place don't you think, Cecilia?"

"Yes. Yes, there is," she said, slowly rising from her hiding spot.

"We might need a bit more juice though."

"Juice?" asked Cecilia.

"For the motor," replied Kuffi. "She's not a carpet, Cecilia, she doesn't run on hot air!"

Cecilia had no idea what Kuffi was talking about and it sounded so ridiculous she started laughing. Kuffi burst into laughter too and both of them felt a great sense of relief. Thank goodness, they hadn't taken Kuffi away. Who knows where she'd be without him, she thought.

6

Juice Boost

They pulled into the filling station just as the Wasp 75 was about to run out of juice. It slowed down and Kuffi had to pedal it into the station by pumping the handle-bars up and down. It looked like hard work but it wasn't for long. The filling station wasn't very big and it was cobbled together using random bits of scrap metal. One lone white fluorescent tube hung low over the pump station, and apart from that there was nothing, no one and no other track riders either. A figure approached them from the darkness within. As it stepped into the light Cecilia gasped.

"Hey, Rosie," said Kuffi, looking up from shining the handlebars. "Cecilia, this is Rosie, Rosie, this is Cecilia."

"Hello, Rosie," said Cecilia, stooping slightly to look into her big, round black eyes. Rosie was pink. A pink chimpanzee-face, with unusual shaggy fur covering her whole body. Cecilia liked the fake red hibiscus flower she had tucked behind her ear. Cecilia recognised the flower because it had been her grandpa's favourite. Rosie was wearing small dark-blue pin-striped trousers and a hand-painted T-shirt that had the word "Lady-Bird" above a badly painted picture of a bird-like woman singing. Although Rosie was about the size of a ten-year-old child, Cecilia could tell she was quite a bit older than her size might suggest.

"Feeling a bit shy, Rosie? That's OK," Kuffi said kindly. "Cecilia's not so bad. She's a friend." He smiled as Rosie began to fill the small engine at the back of the Wasp 75 with "juice".

Rosie extended her free hand cautiously. "Hello," she said in a soft but remarkably deep voice.

"Rosie's a bit of a super star!" said Kuffi.

She looked up at him as she wearily tapped the pump on the side of the track rider and put it back in its holster.

"She's a very talented fruitolin player!"

"I'm working, Kuffi. But the band and I will be playing at El Porto Fino later on tonight with Lady-Bird."

"Fruitolin?" Cecilia began but she was interrupted by Kuffi.

"Lady-Bird? Oh, I can only imagine that will be something quite special. Send her good luck from me, if you get the chance." Rosie smiled a big toothy grin as Kuffi snapped himself out of a passing daydream and handed her a big green button. "Thank you," he said softly, fixing her hibiscus flower so it was just right.

"Pleased to meet you," she said to Cecilia, flashing that toothy smile again; as she turned and walked back into her metal hut, Cecilia saw that she had an instrument case strapped to her back.

"Pretty special, hey? I hope you get to taste her music," said Kuffi.

"Yeah. Me too." She paused a moment. "Taste?"

Kuffi began humming a tune that Cecilia felt like she vaguely recognised. "Can you play an instrument, Kuffi?"

"Ha! No, not with these stubby fingers! Now, let me see, I bet you can. And I'm guessing it's the t-rom-bone?"

"Nope. Not the trombone."

"The flutsical?"

"What's a flutsical?" Cecilia was beginning to realise that Kuffi wasn't making mistakes—he actually thought this was what the instruments were called.

"Well, this won't do. Fancy a trip to the music store? What's your taste in music?"

"I like jazz and blues."

"Never heard of them. I like sweet flavours... My favourite instrument has to be the marsh-cello... delicious!"

"Well, it sounds like we might have very different tastes," Cecilia said, "but I'd like to see what you're talking about... And for your information, the piano... but quite badly."

"Nonsense." Kuffi laughed.

There was a long pause between them as they climbed back on the Wasp 75 and Kuffi got the engine going. They moved away from the juice station back onto the orange line, then Kuffi stopped the track rider for a moment.

"What's wrong?" asked Cecilia.

Kuffi scratched himself roughly behind his ears.

"What's a piano and does it taste any good?"

7

Good Taste in Music

Kuffi parked the Wasp 75 at a junction where the light in the tunnels changed from orange to blue, giving the atmosphere a slightly brown tinge. He pointed at the shop in front of them: Sensational Sound Bites!

"Mmm, let's find out what your taste in music is then!" he said, rubbing his furry hands together.

As Kuffi pushed open the door, Cecilia's senses were swamped in colour, sound and taste. Every toot, strum, bang and briiiiiiiing seemed to have a flavour that accompanied it. A tooting over to her left where a frog-face kid was playing some sort of horn instrument made her mouth water: it was sour, like lemons and limes. She squeezed her eyes tight shut and pursed her lips.

"Guess that's not for you," said Kuffi, patting her shoulder. "Hmm, what about this?" He picked up an instrument shaped a bit like a guitar and a bit like an accordion. Kuffi slung it over his shoulder with a strap. He removed a drumstick that looked like a lollipop and began banging on the squeeze box, creating the most colourful sound Cecilia had ever heard and a flavour on her tongue that made her want to dance. It was a combination of strawberry cupcakes, salt and vinegar crisps and pine-apple juice!

"Yummy!" she said, a smile spreading across her face.

"Yeah, I like this one too! You must have good taste. Shall we go and try my favourite? The marsh-cello!" Kuffi's eyes shone brightly.

"Yes, please," said Cecilia, and she found herself licking her lips.

They walked through rows and rows of curious-looking instruments. They were fascinating objects and many of them looked similar to ones she had seen back home but just when she thought she recognised something, she'd notice it had something extra or different about it.

"You know, Cecilia, there are only a few dwellers who can make flavours by singing? It's rare. But it is possible. Miss Lady-Bird, she can. She has the most beautiful voice and, well, let's just say it has the power to touch your soul and it tastes like tears."

"Wow, I'd love to hear... I mean, taste that!" said Cecilia.

"I'm sure you will. She sings down at El Porto Fino. Perhaps, you'll go there one day." Just then, a heavily bearded bear-face in a grungy T-shirt with the arms cut off, stepped out in front of them.

"Can I help you?" he said in a gruff voice.

Cecilia was struck by the taste of honeydew melon when he spoke, and the flavour rolled around her mouth like a sticky, sweet afternoon in summer.

"Actually, yes. Can you point us in the direction of the marsh-cellos?" said Kuffi politely. Cecilia was surprised: this was one of the first people they had encountered that Kuffi didn't know.

"Head along this aisle here and hang a left at the acorn-dions. Look out along the way—it's quite narrow along there."

He wasn't wrong. The aisle seemed to narrow towards the end so Kuffi had to crouch right down to make sure he didn't hit any of the instruments. At the end of the aisle they turned left and it opened out onto a squirrel-faced girl playing the acorn-dion. Cecilia was disgusted, she wanted to spit: it tasted like earwax, bitter and sharp.

"Quick," said Kuffi. "Let's move along."

The squirrel-face was in her element, swaying from side to side as she played. Cecilia and Kuffi passed her discreetly to get to where the aisle opened out a bit, then he turned and tapped Cecilia on the shoulder and said, "Tag, you're it!" and sped off towards the end of the aisle in front of them.

Cecilia ran after him as a voice zinging with honeydew melon called out, "Oi! No running! This isn't a toyshop!"

They got to the end and Kuffi stood before the wall of marsh-cellos, licking his lips.

"Which one shall we try first?" he said.

"That one," said Cecilia, pointing to a lilac marsh-cello mounted on the wall.

Kuffi took it down, pulled out its spike and rested it on the ground. Then he got something that looked like a tin can and ran it down the front of the strings towards the floor. The sweetest flavours tingled all about Cecilia's tongue: a mixture of Parma Violets and pink marshmallows.

"Such sweet music!" she cried out.

"You're getting it!" said Kuffi as he continued to play. "Grab one, Cecilia, have a go. It's delightful!"

Cecilia turned around and behind her she found a drum-like instrument with a funny-looking bubble on top.

"Yes! Perfect, that bubble-drum will do nicely!"

"What do I do, Kuffi?"

"See if you can work it out for yourself, little thing."

Cecilia examined the bubble-drum and noticed it had a pipe on the side so she blew into it.

"There you go."

A subtle strawberry bubblegum flavour mixed with the marsh-cello flavours, and it all came together in what could only be described as a soft, gooey rhubarb-and-custard flavour. She wasn't sure how it worked and she didn't care—it was delicious! They played for a while and then Kuffi felt they had maybe overstayed their welcome a bit when the bear-faced guy with the gruff voice that tasted like honeydew started looming over them. But as they put the instruments back and made to leave, he called to them and said, "Nice jam, guys. Rhubarb and custard... sweet." He was nodding his head in appreciation. "Yeah, man, you guys stop in again sometime!"

"Thanks!" said Kuffi, who was beaming now.

"The name's Bear, by the way," he said, extending a shaggy hand.

"Bear? That's it? Just Bear..." said Cecilia.

Kuffi nudged her.

"This is Cecilia and I am Kuffi. Lovely to meet you, Bear, but we'd best be off."

With that Cecilia and Kuffi stepped out of the shop, flavours hanging in the air behind them.

"Not so fast," a voice came from behind them. "ID papers, *please*, Mr Kuffi."

Kuffi's face dropped and Cecilia grabbed his furry hand.

8

Finders Keepers

"I hope you've had your licence renewed since we last had the pleasure of bumping into you." It was Julius; Cecilia knew by his sarcastic tone of voice. Marvin followed closely behind him.

Kuffi remained very still and said slowly, "We are just on our way to the office now, as a matter of fact. Don't worry, Cecilia, we still have plenty of time before the office closes."

"Do you know, Kuffi? I think Marv and I just had to close the ID Office down. Some sort of leak apparently. Couldn't be helped." Julius brought the sharp end of his beak up to

Cecilia's nose. "And who, pray tell, is your little friend here? And even more importantly, does it have ID papers?"

"My name is Cecilia," she said boldly.

Julius picked at her clothes with his beak, giving her a once over. Kuffi pulled her behind him out of harm's way, and Julius pulled her back as he continued speaking. "Funny looking thing, isn't it, Marv?" he said. "Where did you find that scruffy little creature?"

Out of the dark beyond the shop came a loud grunt. Julius and Marvin turned abruptly. "Who's there?" shouted Marvin.

Kuffi shoved Cecilia into the shadows and whispered, "Run. Go on, run back to the juice station!"

Cecilia turned on her heels and ran back towards the orange line. She didn't dare look behind her, she just kept running. She travelled quite some way before she got back to the juice station and when she did, it was closed. She leant against the pump, panting, trying to steady herself. She hoped Rosie might come out but she didn't, so Cecilia slumped down behind the pump, out of sight. The lights from the juice station were very low; Rosie must've shut up shop.

As she caught her breath she could hear the scuffling of feet on the other side of the pump. She turned and propped herself up, one hand on her knee and the other resting on the pump for support.

"You lost something?" the voice asked.

It sounded familiar, and unexpectedly a furry hand was offered. Cecilia took it warily, straightening up to find herself looking into the face of the young stag-face boy, Luke.

"Thank you," she said, wiping the dampness from her forehead with the sleeve of her coat.

"Aren't you a sight for sore eyes?" he jested, whipping the hood of her jacket up over her head. "It's probably good to stay covered. You stick out like a sore snout!"

"You won't get away that easily!" A voice came shouting from the direction that Cecilia had come.

"Looks like someone's been up to mischief," said Luke. "Wait, where's Koof?"

"Those bird-faces, the Corvus..."

Luke grabbed Cecilia's arm and ducked back down behind the pump, taking her with him. He threw something over his shoulder into the clearing in front of their hiding spot.

"Shhh," he gestured. "It's a decoy. Just watch, it usually works a charm."

They waited while Marvin's eyes caught up with where the decoy had landed. He spotted it and rushed over to it, instantly distracted by its shininess. Marvin kicked it about a bit, the object glinting in the dim light. It was just a bit of tinfoil but Marvin gazed upon it as though it was treasure.

"That's it, Marv, take the bait," whispered Luke.

Marvin played with the tinfoil for a bit then flew off back off down the orange line. He'd obviously forgotten what he was there for.

"Yes!" exclaimed Luke. "Thank me later! Lucky for us, Marv is a tad forgetful when it comes to shiny things but I guess you'd know something about that, being a wanderer and all."

"I'm NOT a wanderer!" said Cecilia firmly.

"Yes, you are," responded Luke.

"I am not!"

"OK, were you found?"

"Yes."

"Were you lost and wandering around searching for 'the light'?" he said, making rabbit fingers in the air.

"Sort of... I guess so."

"Well then, if you've been off wandering around in the dark for a while and you're finding it a teeny-weeny bit difficult to remember your tail from your whiskers, you are a wanderer. It's nothing to be ashamed of, you know!"

"Oh, were you a wanderer too then?" said Cecilia hopefully.

"No, not me! Jasper," said Luke.

"Oh, Jasper, yes. Kuffi mentioned him once or twice."

She smiled into Luke's silvery eyes "This is all a bit confusing for me at the moment."

"I'll say, but I'm sure you'll catch on. Jasper did in the end," said Luke, tailing off with a disturbed look in his eyes. He was listening out. And almost as if he had summoned it, a shrieking caw came from the Corvus Community, the sound hurtling towards them along the tunnels. Cackling, crackling. "Warning caws," said Luke, standing poised for a second. Then he shouted for her to "get down!", covering her over with his hoody, which opened out into some sort of cloak. He held them down, flat against the ground. A howl began sweeping up the dirt as a bat-face man flew out of the darkness and pressed himself flat against the wall like a piece of windswept paper. A few dwellers who were making their way down towards them from Market Square scuttled along the tunnel, clinging to the pockmarks in the walls and pressing themselves hard up against it. A huge gust swept over Luke and Cecilia; she felt it pressing her chest into the ground as though a heavy ball of air was rolling over her. As it passed she could see it was some sort of air bubble, toppling and ruffling everything in its path—and then it was gone, as quick as it came. Luke burst into fits of excitement, jumping up.

"Woweeeeee, did you feel that!" he said, gesticulating wildly. He punched the air and spinning around he jabbed Cecilia in the ribs. "It's almost competition time! Unreal, isn't it?"

Cecilia was flustered. "What was that exactly?"

"It was Zephira: the wind of sighs. When she passes over she signals the start of the Ride or Sigh competition!" he said, tidying the mess of red hair under his hood. "Gee, Cecilia, wasn't it wicked? I've never actually felt it before!"

Cecilia took a moment to take it all in. She felt overcome with emotion. Happiness and sadness lingered around her like a cloud. It was quite a delicate sensation, like watching a film that makes you laugh one moment and brings you to tears the next.

"Where does it come from?" she asked.

"No one knows really, it just sort of rolls around. Could be ages before we feel it again."

People were just beginning to pick themselves up and peel themselves off the walls, dusting each other off, smiling and talking excitedly.

"What happens now?" asked Cecilia.

"Well, we wait until the sighs start to get colourful!"

Cecilia wasn't sure what that meant.

"You'll see," he said, picking up on her ignorance. "Guess you're back to square one without Koof. What will you do now?"

"I'm not sure. I haven't had a chance to think about it yet," she replied.

"Well, you could come with me. You'd be able to meet Jasper! We both dwell in the same cubby; he might even help you sort out what you're going to do, now you're all alone."

"Really?" she said.

"Yes, but it'll cost you!" he said slowly, as though he were calculating something.

"I've got buttons; how many do you want?" said Cecilia, searching her pockets.

"No. Buttons won't be enough. I want the other thing. The big round thing you had in your pocket, back at the market earlier," he said very seriously.

Cecilia winced. "The marble that you tried to steal, you mean? No way, it was a gift!"

"Fine." Luke began to stroll away, seemingly carefree. "Good luck out there, I'm sure you'll be OK. Let me know if you want to grab some grub sometime."

Cecilia stood defiant as she watched him begin to walk away. It dawned on her that she was lost and alone in a strange place. Without Kuffi she couldn't even get back to where she started. She felt helpless and before she even knew what she was doing she had relented. What use was a marble to her anyway? She caught up with him.

"OK. You win. But you have to help me get Kuffi back as well, or at least help me find him."

"You have got to be kidding me. Are you *actually crazy*?" laughed Luke.

"I owe him," pleaded Cecilia.

"Yeah, *YOU* owe him. I've got nothing to do with it."

Cecilia held up the marble in the light, grasping it tightly before his eyes. Luke stood entranced, his eyes sort of glowing. It was as if the mist inside the marble started to move. Then she snatched it away, this time hiding it in the pocket of her jeans.

"All right, all right. I'll get you as far as the Corvus Community's HQ—the Nest—then you're on your own, kiddo," he said, jabbing his hands in his pockets and rocking back on his heels.

"Corvus Community. Right." She nodded. "And that's when you can have the marble."

"Cool. Deal. Pray on it," said Luke.

"Huh?" Cecilia held her two hands together in prayer like she had seen on Sunday morning TV from time to time—if she was up early enough, that is.

"Not like that. Hold your hand up to mine."

She did as she was told and Luke held his up and pressed his palm to hers, folding his fingers into the gaps between hers.

"Now that's a promise," he said after a moment or two.

"OK. Promise," agreed Cecilia.

"Right then, let's get a move on. I'm tired and I've got things I need to do. I should get home," said Luke. He looked at Cecilia long and hard, then cracked a smile and sighed, a colourful humour gathering about him. "What am I getting myself into?" he chuckled.

9

Layer upon Layer

Cecilia and Luke walked side by side chatting to one another. They stopped to let a group of excited young dwellers pass—they couldn't have been much older than Cecilia, or Luke for that matter. They were audibly excited about the forthcoming Ride or Sigh competition and a young badger-face kept slowing the rest of the party down to show them his moves. Cecilia spotted a goat-faced guy wearing a leather jacket. He looked a quite a bit bigger than the rest of them; he didn't really fit in, and just as Cecilia was about to point him out, he disappeared. Cecilia looked back to Luke once the crowd had faded into the distance.

Luke was tall and broad. He looked quite big and strong but she could tell they were around the same age.

"How old are you?" she asked.

"I'm old enough," he said. His smile was warm and comely; his eyes sparkled even in the faintest of light. Cecilia felt herself blush.

"How old are *you*?" he said, turning his face away.

"I just turned twelve. It's my birthday, well it was when I woke up this morning. If it even is still today," she said.

"OK, but are you sure? Because I can't tell. Who knows what you look like under all that dirt! You could be, like, seventy or something for all I know!" he replied, holding his back as if in pain and leaning on an imaginary walking stick.

"Hey!" said Cecilia, swatting the air, "I'm twelve. That's something I know for sure. All right?" She laughed.

Luke stopped and held the outside edges of Cecilia's arms, looking into her face and scanning it. "Yeah, I'd say you look about twelve... times fifty!" And with that he began snorting with laughter.

"Funny," she said in the same tone she would usually use to annoy Hester. This thought distracted her for a moment.

"Are you OK?" Luke asked.

"Yeah, I just... I miss my sister, Hester. That's all."

Luke patted her on the shoulder. He wasn't sure what else to do. Cecilia trailed slightly behind Luke for a short while once they began walking along again. She thought about Hester and home and inhaling deeply she reassured herself: "I am twelve. I do know where I come from and that I have a family and a cat and a life above ground. I'm not crazy. I'm just lost. I will get out of this place, I will. I know I will!"

Luke waited a moment as she caught up. He could see she was a bit blue; it seemed to hang in the air about her.

"Come on, slow coach!" he called.

Cecilia caught up with him and he put his arm around her shoulder and sort of hung off her the way teenagers do.

"So there's a few things you should know about Jasper," Luke said, matter of fact. "First of all, he's blind. He lost his eyesight in a freak accident, but he's not likely to talk to you about that so don't bother asking. And to add insult to injury, as they say, his hearing isn't crash-hot, but don't worry because he's got this really dorky contraption called an ear horn. It's like the bell of a mini trumpet-crumpet that he wedges in his ear so he can hear you better. I don't think it makes a difference but he swears by it. Fortunately he doesn't go out much anyway. Mainly I look out for him and he listens out for me. We're a team. Oh, and if he's a bit grouchy, don't take it personally. That's just his way. It wears off!"

"Thanks for the information," said Cecilia.

"Don't mention it. Right, now walk on, straight ahead."

"But that's a wall," said Cecilia.

"You always take things at face value. Don't you see that everything has layers?"

And with that Luke ducked down low and slipped away beyond the orange light into a pocket of darkness beyond. A few moments later Cecilia heard an invisible voice calling her name playfully through the wall, sounding like a ghost. She approached the wall with her hands slightly outstretched. Just underneath the glaring light attached to the tunnel wall was a small opening; she could feel the gap with her foot.

"Hurry up! Or someone might see you. Just duck under the light. It's fine, trust me."

She crouched under the light running along the wall; it was bright and marked the insides of her eyelids when she blinked. She moved under it like one might in a game of limbo and shuffled into a cool dark spot behind it. It took a few moments for her eyes to adjust, but when they did she could see another deeper layer of darkness further ahead. Beyond that she could just about make out an entrance not far from her spot in the cool, cavernous space. She walked very slowly towards it and found that it led to a cave within a cave, where Luke stood waiting for her. He ushered her towards an old wooden door, tapping on a lamp lit by several tiny moving lights. He shook it vigorously from side to side and it became brighter and brighter. Cecilia examined it closely while Luke fumbled around looking for a key, and saw that the light came from a collection of small creatures crawling around the inside of the lamp. Cecilia recognised the creatures: they were fireflies.

"Welcome to my palace," Luke said, bowing and gesturing for Cecilia to enter as he flung the door open. She passed through the doorway and curtseyed back. Cecilia let her eyes roam the room. It was quite beautiful, with a black and white checkerboard floor and rusty brass trimmings about the place and panels of mirror lining the interior walls that reflected light everywhere. It was much bigger and brighter than Kuffi's cabin. Cecilia examined the ceiling, which appeared quite low at first. However, when she stood in the middle and looked directly skywards, she could see it travelled quite some way up.

"Who's with you, Luke? I can hear two sets of feet," said an old crumpled voice in the corner. Cecilia hadn't seen him propping himself up by the fireplace; the figure was sort of camouflaged by all the stuff hanging on the walls.

"It's OK, Jasper, she's a friend," said Luke.

"What is she doing in here, Luke? Have you lost your marbles?"

"Actually, I have found them, you'll be pleased to know. Well, one, but quite literally!" Luke said, pleased as punch.

Jasper searched the air for Luke's voice and approached them slowly, adjusting his hearing by using the ear horn hanging around his neck on a silver chain. It was a silver trumpet-shaped pipe—it was much prettier than Luke had suggested when he'd mentioned it earlier.

"Meet Cecilia. She's lost and we have entered into a bargain. I'm going to help her find Kuffi—she's a friend of his—and she is going to pay me with her marble. Quite simple really if you think about it, Jasper."

"Why are you going to help her find Kuffi?" said Jasper, looking rather worried. "Is he lost?"

"Oh right. Yeah, about that... I think you'd better sit down," said Luke.

10

Breaking News

Jasper made his way over to a door that led from the main cavern into another room.

"Come on in, Cecilia," said Luke.

"Are you sure I should? I don't think he likes me very much."

"It's fine. He's just a bit grumpy because he doesn't like surprises, or visitors!" Luke chuckled. "But he'll be fine in a bit."

"I can hear you, you know!" said Jasper.

Luke pulled a face at Cecilia and they followed Jasper into the other room; it was a cubbyhole and Cecilia noticed that there were more doorways that she assumed led on to other small rooms, a bit like how she imagined the inside of a rabbit warren. The floor was covered in rugs and carpets of all different shapes and sizes, colours and textures. It made the space seem quite welcoming, even if Jasper didn't. There were lots of jugs and teapots, plastic bottles, cups and glasses, most of which contained water, dotted about the place. Some were covered over with cloth or saucers and there was one with a plastic top that might have even been the lid from a can of Pringles.

"Thirsty?" asked Luke.

"Yes, please," said Cecilia. The last time she'd had a drink was the tea Kuffi had given her. Luke reached for a small green jar. Jasper piped up.

"You're giving away our supplies... to a stranger... for free?" Jasper grumbled.

"Jasper." Luke walked over to where he had parked himself and knelt before him. Tenderly placing both hands on his knees, he whispered softly, "Cecilia is a wanderer just like you. We're not sure how long she's been gone but she was really lost when Kuffi found her. He's helping her—well, he was before the Corvus Community took him away. It won't be long before he's sentenced by Jacques d'Or and then, hopefully, he'll just have to pay a big fine and she'll be out of our fur."

"The Corvus Community! Oh dear..." A troubled look came over Jasper's face and rested there for a while as the news settled in. "Aww, poor Koof, I can't believe they finally got him!" Jasper's cheeks were red and his face had changed. He turned his glazed eyes to look accusingly in Cecilia's direction.

"So, this friend of yours, Cecilia... This wanderer got Kuffi into trouble? How do you know she's not some sort of spy?"

"Because quite frankly, she looks a bit like you, Jasper, and her story is pretty similar to yours," Luke said.

Jasper began to calm down a bit, mopping his brow with a filthy old rag. "They'll never let Kuffi go. He'll be sent to the Black of Beyond for sure, or worse—you know that, don't you, Luke?"

Cecilia looked at Jasper. He was hunched over and very fair. His white hair was thin and wispy around the edges of his temples. He was wearing a long coat that seemed to have been cobbled together from pieces of carpet. His skin looked almost translucent and in the dim light of the cubby he looked like a celestial being. But he was, Cecilia concluded, definitely a human.

"I never meant to cause any trouble for anyone. Kuffi is such a nice fellow and he helped me when I was in real pickle. I just want to help. Tell me what I can do and I will do it," Cecilia said softly. Sensitive not to provoke an outburst she continued, "He was trying to remind me of who I was. But I already know. I'm Cecilia Hudson-Gray and I live at 141 Enders Road with my sister, Hester, and my mum and dad—Alice and Lyle. Today, yesterday or whenever, was my twelfth birthday. I'm going to be a scientist when I grow up and I love nature and birds and trees..."

83

A bulb of water gathered at the corner of her eye, forming a large tear that rolled down her cheek. She quickly wiped it away.

"What are you doing? Stop it. Don't waste them, you'll have nothing left for the lamentations!" Luke said, astonished.

"Stop what?" said Cecilia, wiping away another tear.

"Stop crying!" Luke and Jasper said in unison.

"I can hear you snivelling!" said Jasper.

Cecilia's eyes were wet with tears and she trembled as she fought to hold them back.

"Yeah, you'll be all cried out if you do that. And then when you're supposed to cry your eyes out with the rest of us to help fill the lake at Polaris, you won't be able to," said Luke.

"What? You're trying to fill a lake with tears? But why?" Cecilia felt a bit dizzy and breathless. "Are you insane? That would take for ever!"

"Err, don't you think we already know that!" said Luke.

"Well then, why are you trying to do it?" Cecilia still couldn't quite get her head around it.

"So we have power? So we can have light? So we can seeee?" Luke seemed to be getting very frustrated at having to explain everything all the time.

"That doesn't make sense," said Cecilia.

"Nothing seems to make sense to you though, does it, Cecilia?" said Luke. He seemed to have become quite fired up.

"Right, you two, that's enough. Calm down, the both of you. Arguing isn't going to get us anywhere. What we need is a plan!" Jasper said, intervening before things got too heated.

Jasper's milky eyes wandered over to Cecilia, and then he moved towards her. When he reached her, he handed her a small rusty jug of water.

"Here, have this," he said. "We're sorry. I can imagine you've been through an awful lot." Cecilia noticed that when Jasper smiled he looked sad. It was strange and made Cecilia want to hug him.

"Drink it slowly now," said Jasper.

"Thank you, Jasper," said Cecilia, cupping the jug with both hands.

"We will be back in a minute. We'll just give you a moment to collect yourself. There are some things I need to talk to Luke about in private if you don't mind," said Jasper. He seemed much kinder now.

"OK," she mumbled.

Luke pulled the door to as they left Cecilia alone in the room.

She perfunctorily sipped from the rusty jug Jasper had handed her...

"YUCK!" she exclaimed, swallowing the first sip of metallic, eggy water. She held her nose and gulped down the rest—after all, she was thirsty. There was a fair amount of sediment that seemed to glitter as she tilted the jug in the light. It pleased her.

She felt better and searching for somewhere to rest the rusty jug, she drifted around the room, picking up bits and pieces. Boy-oh-boy, was it a weird place! There were lots of lanterns dotted about, filled with fireflies like the one she'd seen on the way in. She walked up to one and tapped the glass, finding that when she did the creatures clumped together into a round bulb, which created a lovely warm glow—just about enough light to read a book by. She marvelled at the fireflies a while, feeling sort of sorry for them.

Beside the lantern were many more receptacles used for holding water. One was an old boot with a blue corner-shop-style carrier bag lining it. The boot had a rather bedraggled-looking weed flopped over the edge. It was placed on a mantle over the fireplace, almost identical to the one in the cavern next door, but this one housed a small pile of warm, glowing embers. It had a very ordinary-looking fork next to it, used to poke at the coals, Cecilia supposed. Surrounding the fireplace were lots of tiny pieces of mirror joined together like a mosaic, and each and every one picked up even the faintest light and multiplied it, thus generating more light.

She cast her eyes back to the embers and the scientist in her awoke. Cecilia wondered what the oxygen supply was like down where they were and where it was coming from. She supposed, knowing that an above world did exist, that air filtered through cracks in the rock, but surely they'd need a supplementary supply so far down? Looking at the weed struggling over the boot, she thought about how hard it is to grow things with so little light. Then her brain flipped into worry mode as she considered that the water she had just drunk was most likely full of microbes and had probably been resting stagnant somewhere for quite some time. What if she got sick? Who would look after her?

Trying to take her mind off her worries, she began to make her way towards the door to find the others. But something stopped her. She gasped and recoiled a moment in shock at the figure standing before her. Staring in a mirror, Cecilia tried to make sense of what she was seeing. There in the reflection was a grubby, worn-out little thing, a dishevelled version of the person she had been when she had left the house. She pointed at herself in the mirror and laughed at the state she was in. Perhaps this new look of hers had become her disguise. It felt good to laugh. She collected herself, licking her finger and wiping off some of the dirt. Then she gave up—she didn't even attempt to tidy the nest that was forming on her head.

As Cecilia went to join the others next door, she paused to listen to the muffled voices coming from the other side. It all sounded pretty covert. She leant closer, peering through the gap.

Luke was describing something. "...It's round and heavy but it's not very big. It fits in her pocket," he said. "Jasper, do you really think it could be what you say it is?"

"Don't let your imagination go running away now, Luke. Details, I need details. What else can you tell me about it?"

"Oh, Jasper, it has a splendid way of catching the light and when it does, it looks like something misty is moving inside it. It's magical!"

"Go on..." Jasper said.

"Well, I noticed that it has etchings on it, but I don't know what they mean. They look like some sort of circuit. It could be worth quite a bit!"

"Luke. This doesn't sound like something to be bought and sold. It sounds like the stuff of dreams... but, oh dear me, if it were to get into the wrong hands... I don't know, maybe Cecilia has been sent here for some other purpose that she's not telling us about."

"Or maybe she doesn't even know," said Luke.

Jasper fell silent and stopped the conversation, tilting his head towards the door that Cecilia was standing behind.

"Hello there... I can hear you, Cecilia... Don't just stand there, come in."

"I was just about to come and get you," Luke said, fiddling with his left antler. It was losing some of its fuzz.

Cecilia pushed the door open properly and walked in.

"What are you up to?" Cecilia said, knowing full well. She walked over, continuing to try to fill the silence. "Looks serious to me," she said jovially. Her mood had lifted since she'd had some water. She knew they were talking about her marble and even though she wanted to know why, she dared not ask.

"We were just catching up," Jasper said awkwardly.

"Yeah, we were trying to work out what to do about Kuffi," said Luke.

"Did you come up with any good ideas?"

"Not yet but we will," said Jasper.

"Yeah, Jasper is brilliant at coming up with plans!" added Luke.

II

A Man with a Plan

Jasper leant on an elaborately carved black walking stick bedecked with gemstones that looked like little beetles as he shuffled up and down slowly, thinking up ways they could get Kuffi back.

"We could ambush Julius and Marvin and disguise ourselves as them and sneak in and bust Kuffi out."

"They would have to be pretty serious disguises." Cecilia said, surveying the adorned walls of the space around her. "I don't think we have the time or the materials to pull that one off."

"Not to mention that we'd need a key," Luke added.

"Poison... we could use poison!"

"For what?" mumbled Luke.

Jasper paused a moment and Cecilia absent-mindedly filled the silence. "I'm so glad you found me at the juice station; who knows where I would be if you hadn't turned up. I was hoping Rosie would be there but when I arrived but she'd already shut up and gone."

"Yeah, it's usually open much later than that," said Luke.

"Rosie?" said Jasper. "The fruitolin player?"

"Yes. I suppose it's because she is performing at El Porto Fino tonight."

"Is she? That's the first I've heard of it," said Luke.

"Cecilia?"

"Yes?"

"Do you know who she is performing with by any chance?" Jasper's eyes narrowed; she could almost see an idea dawning on his face.

"Yes, I remember her saying it was with someone called Lady-Bird."

"That's it!"

"What?" said Cecilia and Luke at the same time.

"Kuffi and Lady-Bird grew up together. They are very dear old friends."

"Yeah, childhood sweethearts—until Jacques d'Or came along," said Luke.

"Yes, you could put it like that. Anyway, if we could get you an audience with Lady-Bird we may be able to convince her to help get Kuffi released."

"So, could she persuade Jacques d'Or that Kuffi is innocent?"

"I'm afraid, Cecilia, that he will need a lot more than just persuading. But Lady-Bird is one of Jacques d'Or's prized possessions."

"Urgh, possession? A living thing shouldn't be a possession."

"That's true, but Jacques d'Or sees everything in terms of what it's worth and Lady-Bird has the gift of song and the power to move a person to tears; for a guy who's trying to fill a lake with tears she's pretty hot property. He keeps her at the Nest with the rest of the Corvus Community, which is on top of a tower of egg cells, so he can keep all the delinquent dwellers captive beneath him. Each night she sings evening song to send everyone to sleep and calm the captives who no doubt weep into their pillows. At the end of it she's the only one still awake. So, once everyone else is asleep she could, if she were brave enough, pinch the keys from Jacques d'Or and set Kuffi free. She could then return the keys and go back to sleep like she knew nothing of it and he'd had a lucky escape."

"But where could he go? He can't go back to his cabin— that's the first place they'd look, and they'd kill him for sure!"

"Well, I guess if it's OK with you, Luke, he could stay with us. We have plenty of room and lots of disguises."

"I'm cool with that. The more the merrier," Luke replied.

"But we will need to get to Lady-Bird first," said Jasper, returning to the plan. "We're going to need to get you into

El Porto Fino and that could take some doing... For a start they will never let you in looking like that!"

"Hey!" said Luke. "What's wrong with my clothes?"

"Well, they hardly turn heads, do they? And if you don't turn heads when you arrive, you simply won't get in. That's how it works. You're going to need to look exquisite and I don't exactly have a wardrobe full of evening gowns, so we're going to need to get you some. I happen to be friends with Mrs Hoots, who owns the haberdashery, but she'll never lend them to us and she certainly won't give them to us for free."

Cecilia was a bit lost. "So are you saying all we need to get into El Porto Fino is to dress up?"

"More than dress up—you'll need to dazzle everyone's socks off. Jacques d'Or is a lover of all things shiny."

"OK, well, let's just pop down to Mrs Hoots and buy something to wear that will get us in tonight." Cecilia reached into her pocket and pulled out some buttons and began counting them. Jasper and Luke couldn't help themselves and began to chuckle, throwing each other amused glances.

"What?"

"We're going to need a lot more than that," said Luke. "I know! Why don't we pool our buttons together and bet them on the Ride or Sigh competition?"

"Gamble, are you crazy?"

"What's life without a little bit of risk, Cecilia?"

"Have you got a better idea?" Jasper added.

She sat there thinking quietly for a moment then shook her head.

"But what if we do get to Lady-Bird and she refuses to help? We will have gone to all this trouble and be back at square one. Kuffi hasn't done anything wrong, he just made a mistake and it wasn't even his fault!"

"For Jacques d'Or it makes no difference. If we've got a chance to make it right, we have to try. Kuffi's life depends on it! And on top of that, you're also going to need to be extra careful. Wherever Lady-Bird is, Jacques d'Or and his heavies are bound to follow. He likes to show up and show off, so no doubt he'll be making an appearance and giving some grand speech about how wonderful he is and how much light he has generated."

"Jacques d'Or is out of control, man," said Luke flippantly.

"That's beside the point. Look, I think if we can get you in to see Lady-Bird, she'll help. She'll be heartbroken that her oldest, dearest friend has met with trouble and that she's the only one who can save his life."

"But won't she just think we're crazy fans like everyone else?" said Luke.

"Not if you're not fans at all!" said Jasper. "You're going to pretend to be trainee reporters. She loves giving interviews and she'll be expecting one after she's performed. Once you've gained an audience with her—you can reveal the real reason you're there!"

"Well, Cecilia is going to need ID papers, Jasper, and it's not long before the Ride or Sigh competition starts," said Luke.

Jasper inhaled and let out a big blue sigh. Cecilia gasped as the miniature cloud floated up to the ceiling and disappeared. Cecilia poked Luke in the shin with her foot. "Luke! What was that?"

"Ouch, you doofus, that hurt!" He didn't look at all pleased. Luke pulled in a deep breath and huffed out a deep groan that released a puff of hot orange.

"Oh, that!" he said, smiling mischievously. He waved his hand back and forth through the orange mist until it was gone. "That's a sigh and it means it's almost time for the Ride or Sigh competition!" His voice was getting louder with excitement.

"Yes, we'd better gather ourselves together!" said Jasper, and with that he got up and moved back over to the little desk in the corner and beckoned Cecilia over to him.

"Now then, Miss Cecilia, you're going to need some ID papers."

Jasper asked Cecilia to sit in front of him on the floor. He reached out his hands and felt the contours of her face and eyebrows, lips and nose. It was a new experience to have someone analyse her face in such a way. As he did so she noticed the deep grooves etched into the palms of his hands like ancient rivers.

"You thought I couldn't see you, didn't you?" he said eerily. "But I see things you don't. There's much more to a picture than just paint on a canvas." His expression and movements seemed to have taken on an animalistic style, as had his temperament—no wonder he didn't find it difficult to fit in in this mysterious underground world.

Cecilia's attention turned to the stuff hanging on the walls of the cubby. All about the place were various creations: animal masks, ears, wings and tails. Up close they looked handmade but she supposed that in the shadows one might pass for a sheep-face or a dog-face.

"I know what you're thinking," he said, startling Cecilia. She worried for a second that he was some kind of mind reader, like something from *Star Trek*, which her dad always forced them to watch but which she secretly loved. "My disguises, why I have made them?" Jasper said in answer to the question Cecilia hadn't had to ask.

"Yes," she said plainly, looking over at Luke; he shrugged in return.

"It's easier to try to blend in, I find. I'm vulnerable if I look just like me as I am. You know. A human being."

So he *does* know he's a human, Cecilia thought.

"Oh, is it? Well, I guess I've been lucky. No one really seems to notice me. Julius was a bit curious but apart from that—"

"It's because, to be honest, Cecilia, I imagine it's quite hard to work out what you actually are. You're really grubby, so I suppose you look a bit like a pig-face that's been rolling in the dirt."

"Gee, thanks," said Cecilia.

"Yeah, you'd definitely pass for a pig-face, now I think about it. Anyway what's wrong with being a pig-face?" Luke said innocently.

Jasper agreed. "Yes, your nose is quite upturned from what I can tell but it's still a lovely nose nonetheless." Jasper took his hands away. "OK. We're all done." He turned away from Cecilia and chirpily set to work. Cecilia was fiddling with an old jar that had some kind of specimen in it, a sort of metallic liquid-gel that morphed and changed shape entirely of its own accord.

"What's this silvery stuff? It looks a bit like liquid metal. Mercury or something."

"If it's what I think it is, you'd better put it down," Jasper said, puffing out a small red cloud. "This not the time to mess about with the Deep. Here, look at this instead."

Cecilia didn't know what he was talking about. "The Deep..." she muttered, putting the jar down and walking over to Jasper, who was holding out some documents for her.

"That was quick," said Luke, stretching as though he'd just woken up.

Cecilia looked at her papers. The writing was exquisite, flawless in detail. Then she looked at the "photo" of herself and had to stop herself laughing, which resulted in a sort of stifled snort. It was rubbish! He'd made her look like a oddly shaped potato with electrified spaghetti hair coming out of her forehead. She'd expected it to be one of those magical life-moments where you realise that the guy in front of you is in fact a wizard. This was not one of those moments.

"Oh, wow, it's amazing," she lied, holding back the desire to laugh.

"He's a real artist, right?" said Luke proudly.

Cecilia snorted again and cleared her throat in an attempt to gain some composure.

"Right, one more thing!" said Jasper.

"What?" said Luke and Cecilia in unison—they were becoming restless.

"Some props to support the backstory, of course." He began rummaging and murmuring to himself. "Take these, just in case," he said, handing them some old bits of newspaper. "These are a few old articles from the *Fly*. And a notepad to give the impression you're actually writing an article."

"Cecilia, I can't wait! It's so exciting to see all the sigh riders taking their places at the Concave Stadium for the Ride or Sigh competition—especially if you've never been before!"

Cecilia let out a sigh and a bubbly puff of light-blue steam left her lips. She clapped her hand over her mouth.

"Quick! We'll explain the rules when we get there but if the sighs are that strong already, the competition will be starting soon!" said Luke excitedly.

"Gather yourselves!" called Jasper. It felt like match day as Jasper and Luke grabbed coats and bags. Cecilia looked at Jasper hard and thought about how well he had adapted. She wondered what had made him want to stay there in the tunnels at all. Perhaps he had somehow got past caring about getting home, or maybe when he was up above ground, he had no friends or family and so this was actually a better place for him to be. If she did have to stay down here for any length of time, she thought, at least she had made friends of some kind; and although she was determined to get home eventually, right now she just had to suck it up until she could find Kuffi, who at the very least could get her back to where she started...

Jasper was busy tying on a handcrafted wolf's head. It was a hat with ears and lots of bits of patchy fur stuck to it. It was sewn together beautifully and looked much like the animal hats you can buy in the shops—the fake ones that people wear in winter to keep warm.

"Cecilia?" Jasper said quite seriously. "Please never mention that you have been down here, to our secret cavern, or tell anyone how to get here, will you? Can we trust you to do that?"

"Of course, Jasper, you have my word."

"Follow Jasper; he'll lead us back to the main lines along what I like to call 'Jasper's secret tunnel'," Luke said in a comical voice.

"Great name, Luke. Did you come up with that yourself?" she jested.

Jasper waved his walking stick in the air and shouted, "Follow me!" as he began to feel his way along the tunnel walls.

Cecilia let out a sigh that floated into the air—a thin lilac mist—and watched it dance into nothingness.

They travelled down the tunnel past where Luke and Cecilia had first entered and carried on a while further until a small opening ahead of them showed a dazzling lime-green light. The light danced about, flickering with the shadows of each dweller that passed it. They got to the opening; it was no bigger than a car door.

"We will have to go out one at a time," said Jasper. "So it's not so noticeable that we are coming out from a secret passage."

Cecilia felt very excited and it was clear that Luke could hardly wait for whatever it was that they were about to see at the Ride or Sigh competition.

"You go first, Cecilia. Wait for us on the other side," said Jasper.

Cecilia bent low under the tunnel wall and stepped out into a ginormous hollow bursting with lime-green neon light. It was so sharp and bright she could almost taste it. It reminded her of the Sensational Sound Bites music shop that she and Kuffi had visited, and she felt all the more determined to get him back. The air was electric and she was mesmerised; it pulsed like a heartbeat. Luke came to stand beside her, then Jasper, and she could see in their faces how excited they were too.

"This is the lime-green district, Cecilia, it's where all the magic happens."

"Yeah, loads of famous people come here. They love the lime light and many of them live in this district because of it. Not just anybody can live here, though. You have to be a somebody," said Luke.

"Isn't everybody somebody?" asked Cecilia.

"Well, yes, but you know—somebody... a dweller who's known by everybody."

There was a loud squawk and Cecilia, Luke and Jasper jumped with surprise when a voice called out from the crowd: "Jasper! You old dog!"

12

Risky Business

The jovial voice belonged to an exotic-looking parakeet-face. He looked just like the kind that flew over Cecilia's house when she was gardening with her mum and Hester. He had a red beak and green feathers that seemed all the more splendid in the lime light.

"Augustus, old friend!" Jasper called. He must've recognised the voice.

Cecilia noticed that Augustus was holding a thick roll of old carpet under his arm. He was dressed elaborately in shiny dark-pink coat-tails that trailed off his own tail feathers. There were two rows of medals attached to the breast pockets, placed in numerical order but with gaps in the sequence. Cecilia noticed that this fellow had come first at something at some point and that he had also come fifth, seventh, twelfth, thirteenth and fourteenth. She stopped staring when a scaly green hand with red fingernails, which narrowed to the tips and curled over somewhat, was held out to her.

"Augustus, that's me, and you are?"

"Excuse my manners. My name is Cecilia," she said formally, shaking his hand and looking into his smiley eyes.

Augustus turned to Jasper. "You heading to the Concave Stadium?"

"I sure am, buddy!" he said enthusiastically.

"Nothing like the old wind of sighs to get everyone up and running, blow out the old cobwebs," Augustus said.

"Yes, the atmosphere is unbeatable, there's no denying that!" said Jasper. Augustus laughed and linked Jasper's arm, walking a few paces ahead of Cecilia and Luke, dodging through the stream of dwellers travelling in all directions and catching up on old times.

"Fancy a quick snack?" asked Luke.

"I am a bit peckish," replied Cecilia, thinking of hot dogs.

Luke pointed over to a stand that read The Onion Lair.

"Come on then, while those two are catching up!" Luke pulled at her sleeve. "Oh, look, there's no queue, come on!" Luke said, bursting into a run. Cecilia followed. She caught up with Luke and found him deciding what flavour onion to have.

"Caramelised or pickled? I just can't decide," he said, holding his chin.

A pigeon-faced boy paid and walked off, nibbling at a dried onion on a stick. It looked like a lollipop. Cecilia didn't ask any questions, just sighed, which this time emerged in deep indigo, smoky tendrils leaving her lips like the vapour you get on cold wintry days. She blew it away as she said, "I'll have a caramelised onion, please."

She got a button out of her pocket and said to Luke, "I've got this, my treat. Get one for Jasper too if you know what he likes." The florid pig-faced man serving behind the counter exchanged the button for a brownish onion on a stick.

"Thanks, Cecilia! Good choice," said Luke. "Two of the same again, please!"

Luke and Cecilia returned to Jasper and Augustus who had stopped outside an archway entrance to the Concave Stadium. They were feeling the piece of carpet that Augustus was holding. There was a lot of smoothing down and umming and ahhing, questions about the shape and size, colour and materials. Luke and Cecilia stood there quietly watching before Augustus said, "Right then, chaps. I must be off!" They waved him goodbye and Luke handed Jasper the caramelised onion.

"Here you go. Cecilia got it for you!"

"Oh, thank you, Cecilia. Yum, my favourite."

Jasper told the two of them that Augustus had been sponsored by a big name this year but wasn't allowed to give away who it was. But more importantly because of this he had some inside knowledge on who the winner might be.

The three of them were standing outside what appeared to be a big bowl, which Luke announced was the Concave Stadium. They walked through the archway entrance into a stunning deep, shiny basin covered in mirrors and gold. It was like walking into the centre of a diamond; it reflected the faces and sounds and light of all the dwellers inside it. Luke began to explain how it all worked as he led them to some unoccupied seats. As each member of the audience exhaled, they released a sigh that changed the air pressure and created a colour cloud, which under the specific conditions at the Concave Stadium also contained a feeling. These were what the sigh riders raced on and the audience let out different coloured sighs depending on how they were feeling—technically, they set the mood. A misty multicoloured cloud was growing above the audience, gathering sighs from them as they took their seats in the pit below. The colour cloud swelled as the Concave Stadium filled up in preparation for the competition to start. The air was vibrant and the atmosphere seemed to almost completely absorb Cecilia. She gazed skywards, sighs rising up around her like hot steam. She was lost in the colours and the depth of emotion they held. As the clouds passed overhead she was engulfed in feelings. But they weren't hers: her emotions were being manipulated and she felt out of control until she sighed a waft of yellow that floated towards the colour cloud. It was a huge relief and she felt for a moment she had returned to her senses, until her feelings began to gather in her again as she stared at it.

Luke waved his fuzzy hand in front of her face.

"There will be plenty of time for that in a bit. Don't use up all your sighs now—you'll run out of energy and then you won't feel anything at all when it starts!"

"Oh, right, thanks." Cecilia felt a bit light headed.

There was a lot of huffing and puffing and groaning all around. It reminded Cecilia a little bit of an orchestra tuning up before it plays a piece of music.

Luke looked at Cecilia, his eyes reflecting a lilac tinge that was rising up around them, and he sensed her sadness. Wanting to comfort his new friend, he said, "Here, link my arm." This brought up more feelings in Cecilia than she could have imagined. It reminded her of her dad and going to the cinema or afternoons out for daddy–daughter time. She knew her family would be worried about her and for a moment she felt guilty for getting on without them and not being able to let them know she was OK. Cecilia had lost track of time—in fact, she realised there seemed to be an absence of time altogether. Had she seen a clock or a watch since she had wound up so lost? She returned to thoughts of her family; their faces were fading and all she could build in her mind's eye was a sense of them. She was snapped back to the moment though, when a squirrel-face scurried about in front of her looking for the best seats.

"This one. No, this one?" he muttered to himself. "No, no, this one." He continued hopping about and disappeared only to return with a bag full of rotting horse chestnuts. He sat upright and alert in the seat next to Cecilia.

A shadow passed overhead, casting the kind of moment of darkness a plane does when it flies over fields on a sunny day. This made the crowd hush and the stadium filled with anticipation.

"It's the master of ceremonies," whispered Luke.

She swooped in and landed on a platform high in the air above their heads, cawing a beautiful long, smooth caw that sliced through the anticipation as the crowd stood, clapping and cheering. Cecilia jumped as she heard a loud wolf whistle screeching from a few rows behind them but smiled when she saw it was actually a wolf whistling. He was wearing a faded pink patchwork jersey that had AUGUSTUS THE ALMIGHTY painted on the back.

The master of ceremonies was exquisite. She was sheer black from her head to her claws, even her eyes. She was beautifully composed and eloquently spoken. The crowd roared as the competitors took up their positions. In all the commotion Cecilia managed to watch Augustus take his place in the ninth lane.

"Wow, it's so exciting we know someone in the competition," said Cecilia.

"It sure is, kiddo!" Luke replied.

"But I don't get it. Why is Augustus in ninth if he has already won first? That doesn't make any sense."

"Oh, yeah, right, you need the rules, hey? Well, the whole idea of the Ride or Sigh competition is to get a medal in every tournament, until you have a complete set of sixteen medals. But it takes a while because we never know when the wind of sighs is going to roll round!"

"The wind of sighs... is that blast we had to take cover from earlier?" asked Cecilia.

"Yes, Zephira—it's quite erratic. So the first person to win sixteen medals wins the life-long-sigh achievement trophy. But, If you win in the same position twice, it's a double and you're disqualified from the competition for life and a new competitor is added to the competition in your place. It has been over a decade since the last life-long-sigh achievement trophy was given out and that last person was Madame Midnight"—he pointed to the crow on the plinth—"and that's what your status is raised to, the master of ceremonies. If you double at ninth, say, that's you for ever; you'll always be ninth position wherever you go, whatever you do, and you never get a chance to start over. It's a bitter pill to swallow but those are the rules. You get it?" he asked, matter-of-fact.

Cecilia was still taking it all in. "Yup, got it. But it all sounds quite risky if you ask me. A bit like gambling. What does it mean to have ninth status, then?"

"That you'll be digging tunnels the rest of your life, most likely. It's hardly a coveted position and no one wants to employ someone who comes in late if you think about it!" Luke looked over at Jasper, who was on the other side of Cecilia, sitting comfortably in his seat and soaking up the atmosphere, and lowered his voice to a loud whisper.

"Don't say anything but that's what happened to Jasper. He used to be an amateur sigh rider, then he got brave and tried to make the big time. Turned out he was actually really good. He'd got to twelve medals but doubled at fifteen. He became a tunneller out at the edges of the doldrums."

"Doldrums?" asked Cecilia.

"Gee, it's so tiring being with you. I have to explain everything," Luke grumbled. "The doldrums are where all the waste from the tunnels winds up and goes into composting. It's quite a way away because the gases that come from all the rotting are really dangerous, but it's all part of the circle of life because then that good stuff goes back in the earth."

"We have a compost heap at home. Mum's super proud of it. We chuck all the old fruit and veg, potato skins and that sort of thing on it, but when you take the lid off tiny flies waft out with it and it stinks!" Cecilia giggled.

Luke looked at her and shrugged. He'd been doing that all day. "*Annnnyway*, while Jasper was working as a tunneller he was asked to make up part of a team sent out to search for new sources of water. 'The Water Rats', that's what they called them. They didn't just recruit rat-faces though, so it was an opportunity Jasper couldn't really afford to turn down as it would have got him out of tunnelling and into divining instead. Sadly the day he started there was a gas explosion and a tunnel caved in on him. No one was ever sure how he survived but when he came round he'd lost his sight and his hearing was badly damaged, so he was relieved of all his duties. No one really cared about Jasper after that. That's when we met. I was in a pretty bad state too as I had been abandoned. It wasn't my fault—at least, that's what Jasper tells me. Sometimes it happens, you know. I guess the dweller that left me wanted a bird-face or something. I was very young and alone and I needed nurturing. But that's all in the past now." Luke tailed off.

Changing the subject, he pointed to a sigh rider standing behind the start line, a crow-face boy with a mop of feathery black hair over his eyes. Cecilia wondered how he could see anything. His skin was golden brown, but his wings were jet black. The crowd exploded in cheers again as he entered. Some folk climbed onto their chairs; a teenage hedgehog-face began screaming, flailing her hands in the air. "AUBREY, I LOVE YOUUUUUUU!" she screeched at the top of her lungs. The duck-face sitting behind tapped her on the shoulder, trying to avoid her prickly needles. "Please, be careful with those, will you? You'll have my eye out otherwise!" The duck-face sat back and preened herself, then tended to a clutch of eggs she had wedged next to her.

"That guy there, starting at zero, that's Jacques d'Or's son, Aubrey. It's his first professional sigh-ride. If he finishes at first, he'll win today! There's a lot of pressure on him, and his father really didn't want him to enter for obvious reasons."

"Like?" said Cecilia, probing.

"Think about it, ding-bat."

"Excuse meeee!" exclaimed an offended bat-face sitting next to Luke.

"I beg your pardon. I'm sorry," Luke said sheepishly.

"Yes, well, that's rather offensive, don't you think?" And with that, the bat-face got up and moved seats.

Luke looked rather embarrassed but he continued despite himself.

"If over time, Aubrey doubles at fifteenth like Jasper—or worse, sixteenth—he'll be in the sewers the rest of his life, even if his dad is the leader of the Corvus Community."

"No wonder he wasn't pleased. Pretty bold move by Aubrey!" said Cecilia.

"You bet! This is the most heated tournament I have ever been to!"

A mole-face in front of them with a stack of papers and a feather quill pen interrupted them.

"Did someone say 'bet'?" he asked.

"Bingo!" said Luke.

"No, sir, that's Tuesdays in Market Square. Today now, I'm taking bets on the Ride or Sigh competition," said the mole-face, drily sniffing the air.

Luke and Cecilia filled with giggles and tried not to laugh.

"OK then. We would like to place a bet. We would like to bet on Aubrey to finish first," he said, handing over a pile of buttons he, Cecilia and Jasper had pooled together.

"Excellent," said the mole-face.

"Hold on. Are you sure?" Cecilia said, resting her hand on his wrist a moment.

"Well, what are your instincts telling you?" asked Luke. "What do you feel?"

She stared up into the cloud and let it wash over her. It seemed to be telling her something but not with words; the sighs spoke to another part of her.

Luke nudged her. "Hellloooooo? Anyone in there?"

"For some reason—and I know it's a gamble—but they're telling me you're right!" she said. "Bet on Aubrey to come in first."

"That's settled then," said Luke, handing over one fistful of buttons and then another. He turned to Cecilia.

"That's an awful lot, Luke!" she added.

"Well, let's just say, I trust your instincts... and that's also the tip that Augustus gave Jasper!" he said confidently.

"Brilliant odds, sir," said the mole-face.

"See," said Luke, taking the tickets and thanking him. The mole-face wiggled his nose and shuffled off. His trousers were far too long and dragged along in the dirt.

"I'm not sure how I feel about gambling. My granny always says to stay away from that sort of thing, that it can't lead to much good."

"Sure," said Luke. "But your granary isn't here, is she?"

"Granny! Granary is a type of bread!" corrected Cecilia.

"You're funny," said Luke, patting her on the head. "Technically this isn't betting, it's life-saving!"

Madame Midnight cawed and the stadium was quieted to a murmur. A pale form cut through the sighs that were still gathering; it parted the colourful mists like water and landed high on the stage next to Madame Midnight.

"Is that...?"

"Jacques d'Or? Yeah, that's him," said Luke.

13

Ride or Sigh

Jacques d'Or was astonishingly beautiful. Although he was quite far away, there was something captivating about him. Jacques d'Or picked up a sphere that looked like it was made of glass and held it up over his head. It was about the size of the gym ball Cecilia's mum had at home. She had thought it was solid at first but as she watched she could see it morphing. Jacques d'Or let it go and as it floated over the crowd it grew larger and larger and larger until it looked like a giant bubble full of colourful sighs. Madame Midnight inhaled a deep breath and the audience followed suit.

"Breathe in," whispered Luke, his warm breath tickling her ear, "and breathe out deeply with a sigh when everyone else does."

The entire crowd sucked in all the air around the bowl and the bubble danced before them. Every last drop of air was sucked in until Cecilia's lungs were bursting, then all together they released a sigh, bursting the bubble with a multitude of colours—a rainbow cloud—and the sigh riders were off! The sigh shot around the edges of the stadium. It was incredible to watch as the riders whizzed round on their bits of old carpet, rugs and mats of different shapes and sizes. The sigh riders tried to overtake and undertake each other. Luke pointed out to Cecilia when someone was trying to hold their place in a position as everyone, including the audience, got carried away on this magical wave of emotion. It was like a mixture of horse racing and surfing, and it reminded Cecilia of the tale of Aladdin—he had a magic carpet.

Soon a commentary began, led by a chicken-face and a monkey-face chattering and clucking away from a box at the centre of the Concave Stadium. Jasper adjusted himself in his seat, tilting his right ear towards the sound so he could get a better grasp of what was going on. It was thrilling! When the sigh died down Madame Midnight orchestrated the crowd to release a new sigh to keep the competition going. And the sighs changed colours depending on the mood of the crowd, which acted as one giant being. Every so often a competitor would be overcome with emotion and burst into fits of laughter or floods of tears, shooting out of the loop, then recover themselves and return to the race. It was a spectacle that allowed Cecilia to forget and become completely absorbed in the moment.

When the race ended Luke grabbed Cecilia and hugged her.

"We won!" he screeched. "Aubrey came in first!"

Jasper, who had been quite reserved for the whole event, danced and jumped about too. He was ecstatic.

"Ohhhhweeee!" he shouted. "Right, you two go and collect the winnings. I'll wait here!"

Cecilia thoroughly enjoyed the competition—it seemed pretty simple to follow, but she did wonder if the repercussions were a bit harsh and she brought it up with Luke as they squeezed along the rows of dwellers celebrating.

"It's not like they *have* to become sigh riders. Most of the sigh riders are professionals," said Luke. "They choose to do it and train really hard. Though some dwellers just have an innate gift. Most of the riders are middle-aged and most of them don't have families so they have less to lose. That's why Aubrey's case is such a big deal—he's very young so his father doesn't want him to ride right now. He could potentially spend most of his life shovelling everyone else's poo if in the next couple of races he lands in sixteenth place. Plus, just to make sure the riders are committed, no one is not allowed to pull out of competing. That is, unless you're dead, seriously ill or injured. And if it's discovered that you've sawn off your leg to back out of the competition, like loud and proud Collin McCloud did, that's life imprisonment in the Nest."

Cecilia and Luke perused the crowd until they spotted the mole-face and walked towards him to collect their winnings.

"So once you've entered and been accepted, it's a lifelong sentence whatever way you look at it?" she summarised.

"Pretty much," said Luke as the mole-face counted out twenty-six large buttons into his palm and let out the tiniest puff of a sigh—they seemed to be dying away now the competition was over.

"Then why would anyone ever want to compete? It could ruin their lives!"

The mole-face stared at them blankly. Cecilia stared back and realised moles have poor eyesight.

"Because, Cecilia, it could also change their lives for ever too! Imagine: the power, the influence... the fame!" Luke gesticulated dramatically. "After Jacques d'Or, Madame Midnight is one of the most powerful and revered folk in the entire tunnels. She has a colony of mice at her fingertips and a murder of crows at her feet and she came from nothing."

He paused and watched a few wisps of a colourless sigh fade weakly. As he returned to his senses, he found himself looking into the big round eyes of a bear-face cub. She had a stack of papers roped onto her front, and Luke greeted her with glee. "Ella Bear!"

She looked up into his face; he seemed to tower over her. "Lukey Bear!" she teased back and he extended his hand for a high-five and she walloped him.

"How's my favourite bear-face cub then?" Luke had softened upon the sight of such a sweet, endearing creature.

Cecilia had to stop herself from saying awwwww! out loud.

"You wan' a programme or what Lukey Bear? I'm a busy bear, you know!" she joked.

Cecilia and Luke laughed and Luke made to reach in his pocket to see what they could spare but Ella Bear tossed a programme at them and started walking away.

"This one's on the house for your pig-face friend but you owe me next time, 'K? See ya, wouldn't wanna' be ya!" She waved and smiled as she padded off into the frenzied crowd.

Luke slipped the programme into Cecilia's pocket. "Here's a souvenir of your first race." Cecilia rubbed her nose and watched the bear-face cub disappear.

"Thanks, Luke!" she said, taking it back out of her pocket and looking at the front cover of the programme with its embossed gold lettering and shiny picture of Jacques d'Or.

Her daydream was broken by the sound of a kindly animated voice behind them, and the two of them turned to see Jasper shuffling around and around in a circle trying to locate them.

"You two." He had his silver ear horn jammed in his ear, "Yoooo-hooo, Loooo-uke, Ceceeeeee-lia?"

Cecilia and Luke were mortified. It was like when your mum or dad start calling your name down the aisles of the supermarket and you've just bumped into a bunch of kids from school and you're the only one still in your uniform.

"Oh no! He's got his ear horn out!" Luke clapped a hand over his eye and pulled his hoody further up over his head.

"Nooooo," Cecilia moaned. "Why? I didn't realise he used it in public!"

"There you are! I've been waiting for you, but luckily I've got this handy contraption with me so I could hear you clear as a bell gossiping away! I can't believe we've won, you're definitely going to turn heads with so much to spend at Mrs Hoots'!" He was so delighted it was really rather sweet.

"Thanks so much!" said Cecilia, hugging him. He patted her uncomfortably on the back.

"So now we have just about all we need, the rest is up to fate..." Jasper continued enthusiastically, "and I hate to say it but you'll want to be on your way already."

"Already? But we will miss the pom-pom parade!" said Luke.

"Yes, I'm afraid so but there will be other times, Luke," Jasper replied.

Luke grumbled for a minute until—

"Luke, stop it, would you? A friend in need is a friend indeed. So, I happened to have a catch up with Madame Midnight briefly, and it seems that this whole thing with ol' Koof is bigger than you or I had imagined. She was very worried when I told her the Corvus Community had tricked him and taken him away. So, I think getting Kuffi safely away from the Corvus Community is our primary objective."

"Onto the next then, hey, Cecilia? Mrs Hoots' Haberdashery, here we come," said Luke.

"That's the spirit," said Jasper, patting him hard on the back then he pulling him into an embrace, which Luke did not return.

"Look after one another," said Jasper. It was clear how special Luke was to him.

"Knock it off, Jasper," said Luke.

"Of course we will, won't we, Luke? That's what friends do."

Luke looked a bit surprised but she could tell he was trying to hold back a smile. Hester did it all the time. You can tell because a smile doesn't just happen in a person's mouth and cheeks, it really happens in their eyes.

14

This Little Light of Mine

Cecilia and Luke made their way away from the revelry, leaving the pomp of the Ride or Sigh competition and the pom-pom parade behind them. As they did so a giant bright orb of light came into view.

"What is it, Luke?"

"That is Polaris. The great light," he said.

"It looks like a light bulb, but a really, really big one," Cecilia said, shielding her eyes.

Polaris shone before them like a lonely moon. It was about the size and shape of a hot-air balloon. It had tiny markings etched into it and Cecilia got the feeling it was very old. It looked familiar.

"What sort of energy does Polaris run on?"

"It's connected to the main generator. Sometimes it gets turned off for a bit, you know, to give the generator a rest, to repair faults in the lines. The great thing is the dwellers get a rest too. Everything shuts down for a little while."

Cecilia imagined it was a bit like a bank holiday.

"Why do they need to turn the generator off? Does it overheat or something?"

"Guess it's something like that. Among the dwellers the generator is known as Mr Sparks. Word has it that the generator isn't a generator at all, that it's a... living thing that lights up the entire network of tunnels!"

"That would be a tough job," said Cecilia.

They stood looking at the big light bulb that lit the gaping hollow they were standing in. The air was dry and stuffy, unlike the coolness of the Concave Stadium on the lime line. She imagined the stories of the *Arabian Nights* that she had read with her granny and grandpa and felt for a moment that she was in one of those tales. All around the hollow where they stood the small arch-shaped windows reminded her of beehives. The walls in this part of the tunnels were sandy and dry and looked as though the grains might come off if you rubbed them. Cecilia pondered the sandy floor and thought of the sea. Then, just like that, out of nowhere Cecilia whispered a kind of confession. "I'm really lost, Luke. Like, really lost."

"Maybe you are, Cecilia. I know you think you belong

somewhere else but you don't—because if you think about it, you will always be in the right place if you just let yourself be where you are now. You are your home, that's the way I see it. But don't worry. You'll find your way, Cecilia. Promise."

Luke held out his hairy pinky finger and Cecilia held out hers and they shook them just the way she would with her friends back home.

"So chin up, girl. It could be worse. After all, we are off to get all snazzed up at Mrs Hoots' and just wait until you meet her!" Luke patted Cecilia on the shoulder. He could see she was sad but he could only offer his words as a comfort the way an older brother might.

Cecilia's gaze fell upon people basking under the great light bulb of Polaris hanging over the dwellers below. It was much like the scene you might see on a sunny day in a park above ground. Except there were no trees or grass, no ponds or... Actually, it's nothing like home, she thought.

"It feels warm," said Cecilia.

"That's exactly what it's doing, dude—keeping us warm and sharing its light. We should come back here when we've finished our mission. And just, well, hang out," Luke said softly.

"Deal," agreed Cecilia.

She followed him down a slope and picked up on a musty smell and dampness in the air. When they got to the bottom Cecilia realised that what she had perceived as being like a park was actually more like a beach. It was warm standing in the faint light of Polaris and the soil was quite granular, a brown sandy substance. At first there was no sea to speak of, but as they kept walking Cecilia could hear water and see it glistening in the distance.

"Is that a..."

"Lake? Yeah, people say it's drying up and they're getting in a real flap about it. Jacques d'Or insists that everyone attend a regular purging where we all have to cry on demand."

"Oh, that's what you were talking about earlier when you and Jasper stopped me crying."

"Yeah, no one cries because they feel like it any more. It's a waste of tears."

"It's beautiful," said Cecilia. She felt sad looking into the glittering water. It looked as though it were made of microscopic stars.

"It might be nice to look at but it causes a lot of pain. To be honest, I hate it. It's the worst. So embarrassing. Of course, the Corvus Community don't have to cry on demand; they just stand around bullying everyone else and making us feel even worse than we already do. I've managed to avoid a few times now though."

"It doesn't sound like much fun. Why can't the Corvus Community just let people cry when they want to? Anyway, surely there must be another way to fill the lake?" said Cecilia.

"Jacques d'Or and the Corvus Community believe the best way is to make people really sad, so they'll cry more often. It's beyond me, really. I hate it and sometimes it just makes me angry, then I can't cry at all. But I'm sure if there were an easier way, we'd know about it," he said solemnly.

"But I don't get it. Why do you need to fill the lake at all?" Cecilia spoke tentatively now.

"Well, it's something to do with having enough tears to keep the lights that line the tunnels going. It's all connected to the generator. I don't know, water, salt, a combination of the two is what's needed to keep it going," replied Luke.

"Mr Sparks?"

"That's the one. Well, all I know is it's something to do with how Mr Sparks and the way the light we live by is produced. We have to cry to keep us going and sadly..." He chuckled to himself. "It's just one of those things that you have to do whether you like it or not. Otherwise the normal things that happen all the time like that," he said, pointing at Polaris, "wouldn't happen any more and we'd all be scratching through the dirt in the dark. You get me? Everything comes at some cost."

While Cecilia had been listening to what Luke had been saying, she'd begun to feel something warm in her pocket. She felt very flushed and hot all of a sudden.

"Cecilia, are you OK? You're sweating."

"I think it's Polaris, it's making me really hot." However, the warmth she felt was coming from her jeans pocket and it was becoming too much to bear, so she pulled out the marble to transfer it to her coat.

"Whoa, what's happening to it?" Luke said, almost shouting.

The marble caught some of the light from Polaris and its markings and patterns, mists and spots began to move.

Luke turned to look at Polaris.

"Cecilia! Can you see that? All the markings on Polaris, they're moving too." He looked back at the marble. "Hang on," he said, holding up her hand. "They match!"

They both looked back at the marble and saw that it was beginning to glow.

"What's going on, Luke?"

Luke shook his head.

"I don't know but Polaris has never done that before."

A passer-by, a snake-faced skinny man who looked like an adder hissed the word "Misssss-chief!" and pointed up the hill to where they were standing and started to make his way over to a Corvus Community perch above the entrance to the hollow. The marble began to glow brighter, a gentle light pulsing as the etchings began to move; the mists and sparkled flecks whirled round its interior and a force began to pull it towards Polaris. The marble was reacting to the light of Polaris, and Polaris was responding.

"Whoa!" Luke made to touch the marble but Cecilia quickly stuffed it back in her pocket, a cautious look spreading across her face.

"Yeah, you're probably right. We'd better get going!" Luke said. "Looks like we've started to attract attention." He flipped his hood up and turned and tossed the hood of Cecilia's coat over her head too. The snake-face was looking around for a member of the Corvus Community now and it wasn't safe to stick around.

"I wonder what it means," said Cecilia. "It's like they're communicating with one another."

"Cecilia, I'll be honest. Jasper said he thought it sounded like your marble was 'more than the sum of its parts'. I just thought it would make a good bargaining tool to exchange in order to get me out of the lamentations, or to use as a decoy if I found myself in a tight spot. You know, to throw it to the birds like I did with Marvin. But I'm not so sure that what you have is something the Corvus Community should ever get their beaks on!"

"Well, whatever it is, you can have it when Kuffi is free and back where he belongs. I promised," said Cecilia.

The light from Polaris flickered and the light on the edge of the surrounding tunnels dimmed in response. Birdsong like the break of dawn broke out all around them, beautiful swirls of music, coming from the arched windows as the dwellers twittered to one another. The other dwellers had felt it too, as though something was happening, something was changing. Cecilia and Luke hurried past a smooching couple of lovebirds and a family of sparrow-faces who were packing up the remains of what looked like a rather measly picnic.

"I can't imagine you in a dress! I bet you look dread... I mean, delightful!" Luke joked as they speed-walked away.

"Hey!" Cecilia let out an awkward laugh and poked him in the ribs.

Luke curtsied and started to run ahead, goading her, in between blowing kisses and sashaying down a pretend catwalk.

"Hurry up!" he said. He seemed to be enjoying himself.

"Anyway," Cecilia called picking up the pace, "you can talk! You'll look a right dork in a tux!" Luke sped off and Cecilia chased after him.

15

Hitching a Ride

Luke and Cecilia ran down a tunnel where the ground was lit on either side with two blue strips of light embedded into the ground. The blue light filled the tunnel and bounced off the walls. The tunnel itself was high and almost a complete circle apart from the flat ground, and the air felt refreshingly cool compared to the warmth of Polaris. After quite some distance they slowed down until they stopped completely. Luke leant up against the wall of the tunnel a few paces ahead, trying to catch his breath, while Cecilia brushed herself off, trying to tidy the massive curly dreadlock that was beginning to form on top of her head.

The truth was, although Cecilia might have come across as a bit of a *tomboy* (a phrase that, for the record, she hated), she loved dresses and dressing up. She and Hester could get lost for hours in their mum's wardrobe, parading up and down the corridor, taking it in turns to pose for the paparazzi, but Luke didn't need to know that, or that a little excitement bubbled up when she thought about getting dolled up and going to a fancy place. And boy-oh-boy, would she like a wash.

Luke waved her over to him, dancing in the blue light. "Welcome to the blue line. This will take us all the way to Mrs Hoots and El Porto Fino, where we can scrub up and hear some real blues!" But as he gestured grandly towards Cecilia in a silly voice, a shadow crept up behind him.

Cecilia gasped and pointed for Luke to turn around but he was too busy being silly. A hand reached out from around the corner and Luke turned abruptly as Cecilia caught him up.

The hand belonged to Aubrey and he stood gallantly before them with his rolled-up carpet propped next to him. Aubrey was still wearing his bib from the competition and pinned to it was his brand-new shiny first-place medal. Luke pointed but no sound left his lips.

"Well played," said Cecilia with an air of sincerity and she offered him her hand to shake. Aubrey slightly raised his wings and flicked his hair away from his eyes, revealing one bright icy blue eye and the other black as night. He settled when he realised that the two of them posed no real danger; nevertheless he did not extend his hand.

"Aubrey," he gestured with a nod.

"I'm Cecilia and this is Luke," she said politely.

"What are you lot doing hanging about around here? This is not the best place to be right now. I heard down the line that a blackout might be coming."

"I hope not," remarked Luke, who suddenly returned to his senses. "We are quite far from home. But thanks for the warning, man!" Luke tried to play it cool, shoving his hands in his pockets.

"Yeah, well, apparently Polaris is showing warning signs or something."

Cecilia and Luke fell silent and an awkwardness grew between them and Aubrey.

"So," said Aubrey, "there's still a patch of sigh heading down the blue line. I'm waiting for it now so if you guys want a ride to the end, you can hitch one with me. I've discovered if I add a bit of wing power after the competition, I can often ride the last of the sighs right out beyond the doldrums."

"Outside the doldrums?" Luke was impressed "Right, yeah, the doldrums. I go and hang there sometimes, you know, just to chill and think, that sort of thing."

"Oh, right. I go there to practise every day. I can use the gas pockets. I've never seen you there and it'd be quite a walk. How do you—"

"Anyway, we're headed to Mrs Hoots' Haberdashery. A lift would be unreal, dude." Luke interrupted—he was clearly fibbing; Cecilia noticed that he seemed to have had a personality transplant in Aubrey's presence.

"Cool." Aubrey turned and started to walk away. Cecilia was excited to get to ride on a famous sigh rider's carpet. She looked at Luke and saw he'd already forgotten his cool-dude act; he couldn't contain himself either. They followed behind Aubrey, throwing silent grins to each other. Aubrey flicked out his carpet and it hovered a few centimetres off the ground.

"When I say 'jump', you jump on, OK, guys?" Cecilia and Luke nodded obediently.

"And when I say so, you sigh, right?" They nodded again.

"'Out of sigh, out of time', that's my motto, and these sighs are on their last legs. So we need to be ready, any moment now." The skin around Aubrey's beak curled slightly at the edges and Cecilia realised that for this particular creature that was the extent of his smile.

A bubble of blue mist came hurtling towards them and Aubrey screeched, "Jump... NOW!"

All three of them leapt onto the carpet and Aubrey knelt at the front and vigorously began flapping his wings, stirring up what was left of the cloud of blue sighs below them. "OK, here we go, big sigh everyone—breathe out NOW!"

Luke and Cecilia let out a big blue puff and the three of them were away.

It was a marvellous feeling. Cecilia felt so light and free, the air felt cooler and cleaner somehow and the two watched as Aubrey swayed his body, steering them along the tunnels, his attention completely focused. The people they passed clapped and cheered and the three of them whooped with pleasure as they passed by. All Cecilia's fears disappeared in an instant; she was literally lost in the clouds. She didn't want it to end but when it did, she was shocked and pleased all at once to discover that she and Luke were holding hands.

"All right, you two lovebirds, off you hop. This is your stop. Mrs Hoots' Haberdashery isn't far from here and I can't wait around. This sigh is almost out." The two of them jumped off, landing on their feet.

"One last sigh for the road?" Aubrey called, and it became obvious that Cecilia and Luke shared the same feeling as they both exhaled a mist of pink. Their new friend faded off into the dimly lit tunnel, whooping and howling with joy.

"That was pretty special. I don't think I'll ever forget that as long as I live," said Luke quietly.

"Me neither," said Cecilia. "What a stroke of luck!"

Luke let out a sigh. It had lost its colour already and only the feeling of nostalgia remained. Cecilia could feel it too but it soon passed.

"Right then... Let's get ourselves to Mrs Hoots' for our night on the town awaits and El Porto Fino won't let us in looking like this!" Luke said cheerily.

"Never know, they might have a dress in your size!" she said jostling him and skipping off ahead a little.

Luke looked up. "Where are you going, you nutter? It's this way!" He pointed down a tricolour tunnel that looked like a small rainbow. Rays of blue, lime and pink neon lights converged above the bustling noise of happy shoppers.

16

Mrs Hoots' Haberdashery

Luke and Cecilia walked though streets lined with colourful fluorescent tubes hanging overhead forming dazzling canopies that hung like drapes. There was a lamp tapper up a ladder, waking the fireflies in lanterns that hung from posts. The dwellers around this part of the tunnel seemed idler than those she'd seen before, strolling along, taking their time about things, relaxed and easy.

All around them light bounced off the mirrored windows and doors. It looked magical and quite posh with people perusing the shop windows.

Luke smoothed out the front of his hoody and tucked it into his trousers, licked his hands and tried to smooth down his tufty fur.

"Here we are," he said nervously.

The shop door swung open. "Pfffft," came an exaggerated hoot. "My grubby little angels! I've been waiting for you. Jasper told me you'd be coming but you're late!" The voice came from a puff of white feathers, two huge black eyes and a pointy pale beak that ushered them into the shop and closed the door. She flipped the closed sign around and turned a key in the lock before hitting the lights. A most glorious chandelier twinkled from the ceiling like a cluster of stars, a small cut-glass orb a bit like Cecilia's marble projecting light all about the room.

"That's pretty," said Cecilia.

"Isn't it just?" winked Mrs Hoots, stretching a small soft, powdery wing across her back.

"Now, you'll need to get out of those filthy clothes; Cecilia, you can follow me around to the back in just a tick. First, you need to know the rules. As you can guess, it's taken me a lifetime to source all the materials to make these clothes and I will NOT have some dirty little toe-rags soiling my finery! So hands off! Right then, chop CHOP!" She startled the two of them as she screeched, "What a hoot!", cackling madly.

"Now, you're quite tall, aren't you, Luke? Put this on while I have a think." She threw him a silken robe made of tiny pieces of material delicately sewn together.

"And now come on, Miss Cecilia, follow me."

Mrs Hoots called out to Luke as she and Cecilia walked through to the room next door; her voice was very loud for such a small bird. "Luke, the suit I had in mind for you might need a bit of adjusting. So just get washed up for now and I'll start with Cecilia. I won't be long!"

Mrs Hoots led Cecilia into a small cave of what could only be described as treasure: wall to ceiling trinkets, gowns, dresses, bags and slippers. Cecilia's jaw almost hit the floor as she marvelled at the collection.

"My babies!" Mrs Hoots sang, gesturing to her bounty as she danced along the rails, flicking at the petticoats, skirts and dresses.

Cecilia was in a trance as Mrs Hoots smiled proudly, wafting to and fro, but her prancing came to an abrupt end when she caught Cecilia with her hand outstretched.

"Argh!" she screeched, batting it away, "Don't you dare touch anything with that grubby little hand! There's a wash-basin and soap on the side and towels and washcloths above it... Do not ask where I get the water; I have my sources as do most and it's better left undiscussed. Now, hustle or you won't make it in time for the music!"

Mrs Hoots babbled away, singing and sewing, telling stories of all the famous dwellers she had dressed and styled. She was full of beans and her spirit lit up the room even when she wasn't physically present. She got the two of them ready separately but you could hear her hooting about wherever she was. She gave them each a hot drink that tasted like chocolatey mushrooms, but Cecilia was starting to get used to the weird combinations of flavours in this world so she didn't mind it much. By the end of the twitching and stitching, Luke and Cecilia were quite merry and laughter filled the shop.

"Arms up, Cecilia!" said Mrs Hoots, helping her into her dress. Cecilia extended her arms above her head, looked towards the ceiling and screamed. Above them the cave narrowed into a funnel and it was covered in scores of webs that housed a knot of translucent palm-sized spiders, each weaving away at various intricate patterns.

"Ah, yes, I see you've noticed my lacemakers. There are seventeen of them in total. My darlings," she whispered. Cecilia blinked and stared in wonder as the creatures continued with their work, undisturbed by her outburst. "We share what we catch, don't we, darlings?" She hooted up to the ceiling and the spiders responded in unison with a clicking sound rather like an orchestra of crickets.

Mrs Hoots made some final adjustments to Cecilia's dress and the marble in the chandelier caught Cecilia's eye once more. Cecilia was a little closer now and took a moment to remark how similar the cut-glass orb at the centre of chandelier was to her marble. It was hard to see from where she was standing if it had any of the markings on its surface but the size was similar. Though nothing seemed to be happening to it, not like when they stood in front of Polaris. Maybe just being in the same room wasn't enough; maybe they needed to interact in some way. Perhaps they were part of some puzzle, she mused.

"You're done," Mrs Hoots sang. "Fix your mane then you'll be ready for your big reveal!" she said, clapping wildly and drifting next door to put the final touches on Luke.

Cecilia stood in front of the mirror. Her dress was stunning and she was as fresh as the day she was born—but her hair was a terrible mess. She didn't really know where to begin. First, she tried to find the hair bobble that was lost in the massive knot. Once she had located it in the labyrinth of untidy curls, she began to yank. "Ouuuuuuch," she said as it popped free, and her hair jerked out in all directions like she had just been given an electric shock.

"Are you OK in there?" called Mrs Hoots. "I didn't leave a pin in the dress, did I?"

"No, no, I'm fine," Cecilia answered, smiling at her wild hairstyle.

She stood there pulling the mass apart from the roots and finally managed to part it down the middle, untangling each side as much as she could. Then she grabbed the hair bobble and cut it in two using Mrs Hoots' makeshift scissors. She took the left side in her hand and twisted it round into a bun and tied half of the hair bobble round it. When she was done on the left, she did the same on the right so she had a tidy bun on either side. As she smoothed each side over with water, she thought about how some coconut oil would sure come in handy now.

Mrs Hoots popped her head round the door. "Perfect," she said with delight. "Come on then!"

Cecilia walked back through the partition; it reminded her of one of those makeover programs her mum and Hester liked to watch so much. And boy-oh-boy, did the two of them scrub up nicely. Cecilia stood before her friend in a dress of patchwork lace; Mrs Hoots must've been collecting the scraps and stitching patterns for decades. Tiny pieces of tinfoil and sequins, the odd pearl and diamanté; there were remnants of chocolate-bar wrappers and, well, anything that sparkled in what little light there was had been sewn into each section like faded stars; the dress looked like a morning just before daybreak. Luke wore a midnight-blue suit jacket and a pair of patchwork trousers in different shades of dark green. He had a T-shirt with the collar of an old shirt sewn onto it, and his tufty hair was arranged neatly over the antlers on his head. "You look wicked, Luke. You could be, like, twenty years old or something! I definitely wouldn't ask you for ID!" Cecilia said with mountains of excitement.

Luke laughed. He managed to spit out the words "Nice dress" in return and Mrs Hoots clapped.

"Here you go," said Mrs Hoots as she handed Cecilia a small rucksack designed and stitched in a similar way to her dress.

"Oh, now this is cool. My friends would be super jealous." She beamed.

"What friends?" teased Luke.

"It matches and it's practical!" Cecilia folded all her belongings neatly in her rucksack, checking she still had everything: the marble, her remaining Cherry Drops, an Oyster card, a handful of buttons, a ten-pence piece and the papers Jasper had made her, as well as the programme from the Ride or Sigh competition. In the meantime, Mrs Hoots added a tinfoil bow tie to Luke's look.

"Thank you for everything, Mrs Hoots. I feel like a million bucks... I mean, buttons!" Cecilia said chirpily.

Luke picked up his old trousers and took out a handful of brass buttons and gave them to Mrs Hoots, who smiled with gratitude.

"My pleasure, darlings," she replied.

"Yeah, cheers, Mrs Hoots!" He picked up his hoody and jeans and stuffed them in Cecilia's bag.

"Urgh," she remarked, refolding them properly and putting the rucksack on her back.

"Wait! Just one more thing," Mrs Hoots said as they made to leave for the colourful lights of the lanes. "You'll need these." She handed them both a pair of gorgeous jet-black wings. She looked like a proud mother. "And my work here is done!"

"These wings," said Cecilia, admiring them. "They're beautiful."

"Yes, they're exquisite, I know." Mrs Hoots flattered herself.

"Why do we need them?" asked Cecilia, looking up at Mrs Hoots standing by the door.

"Usually I'm all about trying to look your best and stand out from the crowd..." Mrs Hoots approached them and gathered them both into a huddle, Luke under one wing and Cecilia under the other. "But you never know when you might need to fit in."

"Right," said Luke. "A tad cryptic."

"Now scoot! The work is never done for Mrs Hoots!"

"Thanks again, Mrs Hoots!" said Cecilia.

Luke and Cecilia looked completely different to when they first entered the shop. They were filled with confidence and walked with a proud bop in their steps. Cecilia turned to Luke, smiling, and asked, "Right, where do we go now?"

"Hold on a sec, I've got an idea. Stay put!" Luke bolted into the crowd. Cecilia tried to follow but her dress slowed her down. She called out, "Luke! Where are you going?"

He was back in a flash and he replied, "To get that guy!" he said, pointing to a dog-face walking slowly towards them with a sad look about him. The dog-faced chap looked very sorry for himself indeed and Cecilia tried to work out what was going on. He had wisps of coarse brown and white hair all over him, a stubby snout-like brown nose, big pointy triangular ears, hazel eyes, and a red cravat and a name badge that read WILLOW.

"Where to then, you lot?" he grumbled.

Cecilia paused a moment, looked at his heavy shag-pile rug and whispered in Luke's ear: "Luke, I thought we needed the sighs to ride? I think this guy is a bit loopy."

"You'll see," said Luke as the old dog flicked out the rug and laid it on the ground. Under the back end there was a small black box that looked like a tape deck. He flicked a button and the sound of sighs began murmuring below the machine. A little cloud of blue and violet began to hang around the carpet and they were ready to go.

"Oh, it's like a taxi!" Cecilia clapped and giggled, climbing onto the back.

"It doesn't go very fast," said Luke. "Recorded sighs don't have quite the same power, especially now Zephira has moved on, but at least he'll get us to where we are meant to be. Anyway, it's not far. Just thought it would be fun to arrive in style!"

"OK, where to, cowboy?" said the old dog-face.

"El Porto Fino, please, sir," said Cecilia and Luke excitedly.

"Might have guessed, the way you two are dressed. You'll turn a few heads for sure! Lovely. El Porto Fino it is then. Toot-toot!" And off they went with a lot of huffing and puffing to fuel the way. It didn't take long but on the way Luke pointed out the sights.

A bright lime green, pink and blue neon light shouted EL PORTO FINO above a crowd gathering outside; people buzzed around the entrance in their finery. Cecilia was certainly glad they had got dressed up and she glanced down at herself to check that she hadn't already messed up her dress. In the old days she'd usually be covered in jam or glue or toothpaste by now and her teachers always had something to say about that! Luke paid the old dog-face, who barely paused before gliding on and shouting back, "Don't want to run out of steam! There's still life in the old dog yet!"

As they drew nearer to the entrance Cecilia felt butterflies in her stomach. What if they didn't turn heads, what if they didn't get in? All this trouble would be for nothing!

"Oi, numb-nut, snap out of it, yeah, or they won't let us in!" Luke said, practically reading her mind.

"That's just what I was thinking," said Cecilia.

"Well, don't. Jasper always tells me when I have any doubts about things that, at the end of it all, you're the one in control of yourself and your thoughts; you decide how to behave. Please decide to look like you're really excited about a night out, OK? So, fix up and look smart!"

Cecilia straightened herself, and checked her hair, squeezing the buns on each side.

"You're right. We've got this," she said.

A young rabbit-face turned to look at them and nudged her guinea-pig-faced friend standing next to her. The nudging travelled through the queue until almost everyone in it had turned to look at them.

A strapping horse-face stallion nodded to them and Cecilia and Luke were ushered into the line. He handed them each an entry ticket as they passed, ripping off the stubs. "Nice dress," he remarked to Cecilia as they walked through the archway into the entrance hall.

"Thanks," she replied coyly as she turned her head towards a gentle floral haze of incense that came wafting from within.

17

Another Place and Time

Hester had been asleep. She woke up with her head on her dad's lap and within seconds the world around her came flooding in. There was the gurgle of radios and lots of people in uniforms walking around with a real sense of purpose. A dishevelled man at the reception counter in front of her was dripping with water and speaking in a very loud voice about his bicycle and how much it was worth, saying things like, "Well, what are you going to do about it then, mate?" and "Who's in charge here, I mean, really in charge!" The man on reception was listening patiently and scribbling things down on a form but he clearly wasn't his "mate".

Hester sat upright and looked at her dad, who was resting. Instinctively he opened his eyes and whispered in a hush, "Hester, darling, it's OK, we will find her. She's only been gone a few hours, she can't have gone far."

At that moment the colossal world of the unknown climbed onto Hester's back, and under the weight of it all she burst into tears.

"I know she'll be home soon, Dad. I know it, I know it," she sobbed, heavy drops falling from weary eyes.

"I know it's scary, Hess," he said, extending his arm and folding her into him. "All we can do now is wait and let these guys do their job."

Hester's mum walked over with a tray of hot drinks and Hester noticed that there were four drinks in the cup holders. She smiled in a way that held back some pain but not all of it. She put the tray down, and handed Hester a packet of prawn cocktail crisps.

"I thought you might want these, Hess. You haven't eaten in hours, chicken."

The three of them looked at the tray of hot drinks.

"I thought, you know, just in case she suddenly shows up. I didn't want her to feel left out." Her mum began to sob. "Where is she, Lyle? Why on earth can't they find our baby?"

Hester watched her dad fold her mum into his free arm and she rested her head on his shoulder as a policeman walked over with a man who was wearing normal clothes and looked a bit like a detective off the TV.

"Now then," he said in a serious but uplifting voice, "let's start again from the beginning, shall we? Then we had better get back to the train station and retrace your steps."

18

One for Sorrow

Cecilia stood under the dome ceiling of El Porto Fino in an utterly heavenly world. She felt she had been caught between sunset and the stars. There were small pieces of mirror twinkling above, collecting the rainbow of surrounding light and reflecting it back as though she were standing under a stained glass window on a sunny day. The colours dappled the ground and lit the menagerie of animal faces dotted around her and Luke. There were a lot more Corvus Community members among the crowd than she'd seen before, but there were other dwellers too, some of them wearing wings, beaks and badges to show their support for

Jacques d'Or and the Corvus Community as well. Now it seemed even more likely that he would make an appearance.

"I think it's time to put on the wings Mrs Hoots gave us, Luke."

"Not a bad call. I think Mrs Hoots was right: we don't want to stand out too much now we're in," Luke replied. "It's wicked though, isn't it? I've heard about it but I've never seen it before. I can't believe we got in!"

A muffled horn sang out, soothing the crowd to a hush, and they stood waiting for something to happen. The lights faded to a spotlight on the centre of a stage a few feet in front of them, and Cecilia and Luke saw a beautiful brown bird-faced woman with a golden beak saunter onto it. Cecilia fell immediately under her spell.

"That's Lady-Bird," Luke muttered to Cecilia, not taking his eyes off where she was standing onstage. Waiting for Lady-Bird to do something sent shivers running down Cecilia's spine, like when someone hits the tickly spot just behind your ear with their breath. Gasps and whoops were thrown out from the audience sporadically, and Lady-Bird acknowledged these with grace, a slight nod of her head, her bronzed beak glowing before she opened it to release a flute-like call into the dome. It reverberated off the roof and into the ears of the audience, who were instantly lulled by the soaring tone of her voice that brought the taste of the sweetest tears to their lips.

"This is my one for sorrow..." Lady-Bird said to the audience in a soft, sultry voice, but before she began to sing three more spotlights fell upon the stage, revealing a cow-face on the marsh-cello, a sheep-face holding a set of brushes to play the bubble-drum and finally, a face Cecilia recognised: there was Rosie standing on the stage, trembling hugging her fruitolin tightly to her chest. Lady-Bird began:

> *"This is my one for sorrow…*
> *Because I've found no room for joy*
>
> *I was just a girl*
> *Back when I met my boy*
>
> *And as my threads turn slowly silver*
> *All I have is this tune to hold*
>
> *Cos love's dream is worthless*
> *In a world made of glitter and gold*
>
> *And so I'll always keep my secret and swear,*
> *it's never to be told*
>
> *For this, is my one for sorrow…*
> *And the only friend I'll ever know."*

There was utter silence when Lady-Bird finished singing and a stilling of time took place before applause rose up around the room like a fierce fire. She bowed and her dress, Cecilia now noticed, was entirely fashioned from… rusted ring pulls and old milk-bottle tops like the old-fashioned ones Granny ordered from the milk man! Aghast and pointing, her voice raised from a mutter against the din of the crowd…

"Her dress... Luke, we have them back home! It's made from old milk-bottle tops... And ring pulls from drinks cans!"

She tugged on Luke's jacket; his face was in rapture. "I know, isn't she mesmerising?" he said, nodding furiously.

Cecilia made to push herself forward but Luke grabbed her and held her back, "Where are you going?"

"The show's over. We need to get to her, don't we?" Cecilia said, her voice just above a whisper.

Then it dawned on her that the crowd was extremely full of Corvus. All around them the other dwellers began putting on pairs of jet-black wings—those who weren't wearing them already or who hadn't had them since birth, that is. It was then Cecilia really understood how important it was that Mrs Hoots had given them the wings to wear: because everyone else was wearing them to show their support and without them they might have been seen as opponents.

"Cecilia, I'm sorry. It's not safe, just look around you," he whispered. "You can't just wander off, this is about to get serious. We will find Lady-Bird after. It looks like something is about to happen right here, right now."

"You're right. Thanks, Luke. I just feel so awful—I want so much to help Kuffi."

"I know you do," said Luke, "but one step at a time, OK?"

A band of bird-faced figures stepped out from the shadows and lined up on the stage while Lady-Bird was escorted off into the wings by a grumpy-looking goose-face.

Abruptly a violent cawing call broke out, shattering the peace left by Lady-Bird. A rhythmic crackling cackle and a fervent flapping of wings moved the air around the room in a flurry. Fear washed over Cecilia, and she broke a sweat as if waking up from one nightmare to find herself in another. Through the band of crows emerged the magnificent and unmistakable form of Jacques d'Or.

As he came into view Cecilia's jaw gaped a little. She realised Jacques d'Or wasn't made of gold; he was an albino magpie, with beautiful ruby-red eyes. Cecilia could tell he was a magpie from his shape. She'd always loved magpies! However, he was unlike all of the rest of the dwellers that Cecilia had encountered on her journey through the tunnels: Jacques d'Or had no other human body parts apart from his arms—it was as though they had just been stuck onto him under his wings—other than that he was a man-sized golden bird. No wonder everyone thought he was special; he was a very rare and wonderful sight to behold. He shone against his dark shadow, a giant stretched out behind him on the back of the stage. His voice commanded:

"Brothers, sisters and friends among us here today. They said it couldn't be done, but I have never believed in the impossible. If I can imagine it, if I believe it, then the nothing can stand in our way! We possess the true power of darkness: FEAR!

"We have the dwellers under our command now and for ever! Join me!" He roared, his voice ricocheting off the ceiling, shaking the heaven above their heads as he began to chant, the crowd joining in with him:

"Fear is no foe,
He's a friend of mine,
Who keeps the weak in check and the rebels in line!"

Cackling broke out all around the room. It sounded like the poisonous laughter of scores of witches in the scary movies that Cecilia wasn't really allowed to watch. She stood rooted to the spot. Jacques d'Or shot into the air and wafted over the crowd, extending his strange lanky arms to high-five the crowd below him. They exploded into a cacophony of encouragement. He returned to the stage, composed himself and, grinning and with grand gestures, he continued.

"Many of you in attendance here today have come to me at some time of need and asked me to ease your pain, your suffering, to help you feed your family or to wet your mouths. You've asked me to bring about change. But I am not the one who'll line your pockets. I'm not the worms on your table. I cannot continue to be the shoulder to catch your tears! If you want us to expand as a community, the Corvus Community, you must learn to stop your snivelling and come to me with ambition and ideas. We have to continue to be the driving force that leads the way in the darkness. *Carpe noctem!*"

The whole room exploded in response, "*Carpe noctem!*"

Cecilia realised she was gripping Luke's hand very tightly. There is nothing quite like an unfamiliar rowdy crowd to make you feel out of place, like when you sit in the other team's stands at the football, she thought. The crowd settled and when Jacques d'Or's voice rose once again, she wished he would stop.

"We must build from the bottom up. It is important that you all understand that the state of having little or nothing is actually a blessing, not a curse. You see now we can design our new future! What we need to do now that we have harnessed the power is to control it. But how? Let me introduce our honorary speaker, Violet."

A big hunched crow shuffled slowly forwards from the Corvus Community banner lining the stage behind Jacques d'Or. Cecilia had not noticed her before. Her feathers were tattered and patchy, reminding Cecilia of when she found her favourite jumper had been munched by moths over a particularly warm summer. Violet's presence hushed the crowd and she began.

"The Corvus Community has worked tirelessly at trying to find ways to bring more light through to the furthest reaches of this great intricate network of tunnels in which we dwell. And the system we have come up with has not only proved to be a success, but we have found new ways to generate more light and keep the growth of the Black Forest circulating clean air around our system. However, as the lake below Polaris—the lake of light—continues to shrink, it has become even more important to encourage a sombre tone among the dwellers so that they will increase their production of tears to refresh the supplies that support the function of Mr Sparks—our generator."

There was an outbreak of chatter among the audience.

"Please, please, calm your beaks." Silence fell once again. "As a result we have decided we need to bring morale down to an all-time low in order that the output of tears is higher and the lake fuller, and thus, the light of the tunnels generated by Mr Sparks brighter. To do this we have devised a plan to put an end to the Ride or Sigh competition, to shut down all luxuries and to permit only what is necessary to sustain life among the dwellers. In the meantime, to enhance the wave of sorrow we are going to take hostage key figures of the community. You know the types I am talking about. They are the do-gooders, the respected figures, the creatives, the poets and the sigh riders, the folk who..."

Violet paused dramatically, ensuring she was in complete command of the crowd.

"...bring the dwellers hope!" she finished with disdain.

Applause and a chorus of caws broke out, shaking the dome above their head. Black shadows jumped into the air, swooping all around, screeching.

"Of course, we will look after our own, and committed Corvus Community members will receive ample opportunity to prove their worth and be rewarded for it. Just as these next two have." Violet flicked her head in a robotic fashion and Julius and Marvin stepped forward into the spotlight. Cecilia bubbled with rage as Violet began commending them on their "good work" and retold the story of how they had captured Kuffi. Enraged, Cecilia fought the urge to boo and hiss. The situation forced her to listen to what Violet had to say.

"Julius and Marvin found a certain somebody's ID papers were due for renewal. Using this knowledge they closed the ID Office early because they feared there might be some sort of gas leak." Violet gasped for effect. Cecilia could hardly bear to listen to the lies. "The cunning Corvus," Violet continued, "then sought out the offending party and rechecked the papers. As the office was now closed that dweller could no longer renew their ID papers before they went out of date, and Julius and Marvin were forced to bring the offender in and hold him at the Nest!"

Violet stalked the stage, then swept back into the spotlight.

"This is the kind of initiative we expect from you, the Corvus Community! What a cunning plan! Now let's employ this as a method to control. We decide who stays and who goes, and all the while we are still keeping the peace and protecting the dwellers. How often do dwellers really check their papers? We have cleverly made copies of invalid documents to be switched with the originals on point of contact with these 'respected' types for the very purpose of removing them from our society altogether in the coming months. Because without these 'role models' we can bring morale right down to an all-time low. Let's extinguish hope, for without hope there is only grief, and the greater the grief... The greater the relief... MORE FEARS FOR TEARS!"

Violet screamed and to Cecilia's and Luke's terror the crowd roared the slogan back over and over so they too were compelled to do so. Even if they didn't agree with it, they did not want to stand out in this crowd. Cecilia felt incredibly sad. She tried not to show it, but it was at that point that she knew their plan would work to make the dwellers sad too.

"Thank you, Violet," Jacques d'Or said, hopping in and tapping her on the shoulder to reclaim his spot centre stage.

"More fears for tears," he said plainly.

The crowd went wild. Jacques d'Or smiled, beaming with pride, and stood there soaking up the atmosphere.

"The unhappier our society is the more the dwellers will cry. Nothing grows in the dark except the Corvus Community. We will make history here today, remember that! We are the shadows and it is the shadows that control the light! Let's give you a good example of the type of dwellers we will be looking to remove. Bring them on, guys!"

At this point Kuffi and Madame Midnight were escorted onto the stage. Luke visibly clenched his jaw and his nostrils flared; tears edged Cecilia's eyes, and she pulled a fake smile to try to mask her heartbreak.

"Welcome the first of our 'missing' dwellers," said Jacques d'Or. There were a few gasps of surprise and delight dotted about the audience. "We will hold them in the Nest for the next few weeks and when they are at their weakest, lowest point, we will send them to the doldrums where we'll let the gas explosions deal with them—or worse still, they'll wander off into the Black of Beyond... FOR EVER! The likelihood of their survival is next to none. During which time we will explain to the rest of the dwellers that the dark is encroaching and that it has swallowed them up and will eventually consume us all if they don't commit to more weekly lamentations. This will keep Mr Sparks in good running condition and help to generate more power that we can more easily control. Every time the dwellers begin to cheer up we will bring them right back down by simply picking off another unsuspecting 'role model'. Meanwhile, we can rest on our perches and continue our surveillance from the darkness—keeping the order!"

Cries and flapping broke out.

Cecilia saw Luke's lips mouthing something; Kuffi was looking at him from the stage. The cables wrapped around Kuffi and Madame Midnight were pulled and they were jolted into walking off the stage.

As she was torn away, Madame Midnight called out in fury, "My murder will come for you, Jacques." She spat on the ground after she said it. "You'll see, my murder will come for you!" Julius grabbed her by the beak and they were gone.

The crowd was roaring and Jacques d'Or stood with his wings raised, soaking it all up. Cecilia thought he looked a bit like a famous pop star and shuddered as she remembered that he definitely was not. Pop stars sung of love and happiness. Jacques d'Or's song was one of fear and sadness but Cecilia knew that of all things, she must not lose hope.

19

Lady-Bird, Lady-Bird

At the end of the meeting the animated crowd filtered out chattering among themselves, apart from a few stragglers who hung about trying to get autographs. It seemed that everyone was so absorbed in their chats that they hardly noticed Cecilia and Luke standing in the middle of it all.

Cecilia saw a flash of glittery ring pulls pass by the bar and grabbed Luke by the hand.

"Come on, I've just seen the Lady we came here for!"

"Well, well, well! What do we have here?" A croaky voice attached to a long white-feathered neck dropped down to eye level, blocking their way, a black bead of an eye surveying them.

"Two little rebels, dressed up to the nines, it seems. The name is Blanche and I'm the proprietor of this place. What business have you here?"

Blanche had a somewhat spicy personality and Cecilia could feel the heat of interrogation prickling her skin. Cecilia unzipped her backpack and rummaged around before whipping out the notepad and the newspapers that Jasper had given them.

"Such a pleasure to meet you. We are trainee reporters, Miss Blanche, here to interview Lady-Bird, if we may?" she said with conviction.

"Oh, I see, and who sent you?" Blanche said suspiciously, flicking her head sideways.

"We are from the *Fly*, ma'am," Luke said in lightning-flash response.

"Well, why didn't you say so?" Blanche had no idea who they were but her pride wouldn't let her show it. "Follow the bar round to the entrance hall, cut diagonally across from it, and it's the mirrored door on the left."

The two made to leave right away but that was premature; Blanche's voice stopped them in their tracks again.

"Just wait one second. I don't recognise..." She teetered on the edge of finishing her sentence and Cecilia's blood ran cold. "You. Come here," she said, beckoning Cecilia with a menace dancing around her eyes. "I don't recognise that design."

Cecilia looked down at herself.

"That's a very splendid dress. Where did you get it from?" Blanche enquired.

"Mrs Hoots' Haberdashery," Cecilia stuttered. She was trembling so much she held her hands tightly in front of her to stop it from showing. Blanche reached out her own hand and ran it over the lacework.

"Yes. It's quite lovely. I should've known. OK, now scoot," she huffed. "I have business to attend to." And she turned on her heels, gliding off through the last remaining dwellers.

Luke looked at Cecilia and almost laughed, but he didn't make a sound, just wiped his brow, and they scuttled off around the bar.

At the back of the entrance hall was a small embellished mirror door. Perhaps it had once been an actual functioning mirror, but years of grubby hands pushing it open had left it looking old and spotted. Cecilia winced as a memory of her mum flashed before her, like a bolt of lightning, and she felt hot and frustrated. Mum would have called it "vintage", she thought and in this case she would probably have been right. Luke tried the door by gently pushing on it and it opened. They were both surprised that it was unlocked. They hesitated a moment but some shouting behind the bar made them jolt into action and they slipped through to the other side.

The entire room was made of mirrors of all different shapes and sizes and of varying degrees of reflectiveness. As they walked into the room, they saw a multitude of images of Lady-Bird and her voice rang out tunefully, but they could not tell which one, if any, was actually her.

"Can I help you," she asked. "Are you lost?"

"No," said Cecilia. "You are just the Lady we are looking for."

"What do you want?"

"We are here to interview you, Miss Lady-Bird," said Luke.

"Oh, you're from the *Fly*, then?" said Lady-Bird. "I've been expecting you—although you're not who I was expecting to interview me. Give me a moment and I'll be right with you."

"You know they say, never meet your heroes, Luke, so prepare to be disappointed," whispered Cecilia.

Luke frowned and made a shushing noise then turned to Cecilia. "How do I look?"

"Smashing," she replied. "And me?"

"Fine," he said, pulling a feather out of her hair, completely unaware that he was doing so. He held the feather up to the light and blew it away softly. Cecilia broke his reverie.

"I hope that the *Fly* haven't sent any other journalists to interview Lady-Bird today. Gee whiz, I wish she'd hurry up!"

"Yeah, well, I bet the real journalists wouldn't be telling anyone the truth about what was actually said in that speech or what Jacques d'Or is actually planning to do."

"Technically nor will we, Luke."

"Oh yeah," Luke said, scratching his chin.

"Here she comes," hissed Cecilia, smoothing down the skirt of her dress.

Lady-Bird moved slowly as though she considered every gesture seemingly part of some larger dance. Her feathers were exquisite, softly echoing the tones of fallen leaves in autumn, and her poise unmatched by anyone Cecilia had met during her time with the dwellers. Luke was speechless in her presence.

"I've ordered you some tonic," she said. "It'll be along in a minute. It's the best, of course!"

"I bet!" said Luke awkwardly. Cecilia nudged him.

"So what would you like to know?" said Lady-Bird. Her voice was like a deep velvet blanket edged with the tinkle of diamonds knocking against one another.

"Well, actually," said Cecilia, "we wanted to do something a bit different to what you might be used to."

"And what might that be?" asked Lady-Bird.

"We want to talk about the truth," said Cecilia.

"Everyone always wants the truth," said Lady-Bird, repositioning herself.

"Well, actually it's us who want to come clean but we don't want to alarm you. We believe we have a common interest and that you might be able to help us save our friend."

Lady-Bird sat very still. It was extremely hard for Luke or Cecilia to gather what she might be thinking from the expression on her face or her body language.

"I'm listening," she said finally.

"Some of the things that Jacques d'Or said about making people feel sad all the time, and the way he wants to do it, aren't right," said Luke, taking over.

"Cecilia and I have been trying to come up with a plan to help Kuffi get freed but after tonight it looks like we'd be heading straight for the Nest ourselves if we were to speak out. So we need your help more than ever."

"Oh now, look here. Jacques d'Or is not the kind of magpie-face you want to interfere with. It's not a good idea to mess with the man in charge, trust me; he will only bring you sorrow," said Lady-Bird, hanging her head slightly.

Cecilia leant in and said softly, "It's OK to be sad sometimes and because you feel it, but it's not right for someone to make you sad all the time and for the Corvus Community to enjoy that sadness and benefit from it."

"You don't understand," said Lady-Bird, getting up. "We need to keep Mr Sparks going. Without him, there will be nothing left."

"But what about your friends, Kuffi and Madame Midnight? He's going to put them in the Nest and then dispose of them for ever. If we let them do this now, what will there be left to hope for? They'll keep on until there's nothing left. And who will be there to defend you when everyone else is gone?" Luke's words were heavy with honesty.

Lady-Bird sat back down. "You're just kids," she said, shaking her head. "You know you shouldn't go poking your beaks into matters that don't concern you. Someone might get hurt—or worse, killed!"

"But that's just it. Before it was just Cecilia and me that it concerned—we just wanted to rescue Kuffi—but after tonight's revelations, we've realised it's a matter that concerns all the dwellers. We are going to be slaves to Jacques d'Or's commands and you're right, someone is going to be killed starting with: Kuffi and Madame Midnight," Luke said.

"But what can I possibly do?"

"You're the only one with access to the Nest," said Cecilia, "and the only one close enough to Jacques d'Or to be trusted."

"Impossible. Even after evening song it's so bright in there someone is bound to see me."

Cecilia looked at Luke and Luke looked at Cecilia, and then they both looked at Lady-Bird.

"You have got to be kidding," she said incredulously.

"Will you help us or not?" asked Cecilia.

Lady-Bird threw back her wings and clapped her hands. A llama-face lady entered the room. "Lady Llama, bring me a change of clothes and make them inconspicuous. I have some business to attend to."

20

Twists and Turns

They left El Porto Fino and entered the cool, damp air of the tunnels. Cecilia and Luke waited for Lady-Bird as she waved goodbye to the horse-faced stallion at the door. "See you tomorrow, Salvatore." He nodded goodbye and Lady-Bird joined their company.

"Lady-Bird," said Cecilia. "I hope you don't mind me asking and maybe you don't know... but what is Mr Sparks? Is it a real living thing or just a big electricity generator?"

Lady-Bird stood before them, wrapping a black and white polka-dot scarf around her head and tying it in a bow under her beak as she spoke, "You know that buzzing you hear?" Luke nodded. "The long, constant hum that you can hear if you stop, pay attention and just listen?" They all stood listening; it sounded like an old fridge to Cecilia. "If you think about it, you realise it's always been there, a low hum that is in sync with the pulsating flicker that comes from the lights especially when they're low?"

"Yes..." Cecilia and Luke said in unison.

"Well, that's him, but he's not a machine. Mr Sparks is an ancient living thing. He's the heart of our system, pumping light along all the tubes that light up all the tunnels: one big living electric circuit. We all have that flicker within us but Mr Sparks, he's *special*."

"Have you seen him?" Luke asked. He had the eyes of a child being told a ghost story.

"No, but I do know where he is. The generator room is not too far from the Nest, if you follow the edge of the Black Forest north. To be honest, when I had my chance to see Mr Sparks, I was afraid to look. Jacques d'Or took me to him once. He invited me inside beyond a huge iron door, and although apparently Mr Sparks is truly beautiful—perhaps the most beautiful shining thing Jacques d'Or could get his beak on—I couldn't bear to see a living thing captured and tortured in such a way." With that she put on a pair of shades that looked as though they might belong to some old swimming goggles held together with stiff pieces of wire.

"So, how do we shut down a living thing without killing it? I assume we have to switch the generator off somehow to create a blackout," said Luke.

"It's going to be tricky but I know it has something to do with draining the main tank." Lady-Bird's voice quivered with distress. "The poor thing, Mr Sparks deserves better. I wish we could release him back into the lake where he belongs. But as he is the only source of light for the entire network of tunnels, we can't. If we can get to him and drain the tank that keeps him prisoner, at least we can create a blackout while the tank refills. That should buy us a few minutes.

"We're in big trouble if one of us gets caught. The hardest part is going to be getting you two past the guards and inside the generator room to Mr Sparks, so that I can let Kuffi out of the Nest," said Lady-Bird.

"And Madame Midnight," said Luke. "Once she tells everyone what happened to her, there'll be a revolution!"

"Calm down, Luke, we've a long way to go yet," said Lady-Bird, "and I'm afraid we are going to have to split up to put our plan into action. Unfortunately I can't be in two places at once."

"OK," said Luke.

"There's a lot the dwellers don't know about Jacques d'Or. His looks aren't the only reason he's called that. He's a collector of shiny things and he stows them away like treasure. He is sitting on a pretty big stash, underneath the Nest! That creature is a greedy thief! That's why everyone trades in buttons; he's obsessed with keeping all that shines to himself and his greatest admiration is for light itself. To light himself up and turn him gold. That's why the Corvus Community exist: they are attracted to him instinctively. No one knows he's just a plain old bird-face like anyone else. He's managed to trick everyone into believing he is what's valuable.

"We can't just break into the Nest and snatch Kuffi from underneath him in plain sight because perched overhead and guarding the almighty Jacques of gold himself will be several of his heavies, the main guards of the Corvus Community. They're his servants, don't forget."

"Do they know about all that treasure?" asked Cecilia.

"Of course not," replied Lady-Bird. "They think Jacques d'Or *is* the treasure—that he's special."

Cecilia's thoughts were racing as she stood there taking in what Lady-Bird was saying. She knew there was one piece of treasure Jacques d'Or didn't have. Her marble.

Lady-Bird looked over her shoulder to check no one was eavesdropping.

"When we turn off Mr Sparks, Jacques d'Or will be rendered powerless to do anything—at least until the lights come back on—and by then Kuffi and Madame Midnight, if I can release her too, will be long gone. When Madame Midnight breaks the news, like Luke said, there will be a revolution."

"What will you do, Lady-Bird?"

"I don't know but I'm never going back there if all this works out. This is it, my moment to break free. Finally I'll be able to sing when I want to. I won't just be a lame warm-up act as an introduction for Jacques d'Or and his gang."

"And Mr Sparks?" added Cecilia but before anyone could find the answer, the horse-face stallion from the door at El Porto Fino approached them.

"Are these two bothering you, Miss Lady-Bird?" he said.

"No, they're fine, Salvatore. We're just heading off actually. Thank you."

The horse-face walked slowly back to his spot under the luminous sign.

"I think we'd better go," said Lady-Bird. "We can grab a cup of hot liquorice tea on the way."

"Yum!" said Luke.

21

Hole in the Wall

Cecilia felt she was getting used to how the tunnels worked. Each one was connected to an opening, a plaza of some sort, that would lead on to another tunnel leading somewhere else. It felt reassuring to understand how it all worked. Luke, Lady-Bird and Cecilia travelled along a tunnel that could just about fit a double-decker bus inside it. Here the light shone down from above, one thick red strip, and the sides of the tunnel were tiled in black and white checks.

"Cool," said Cecilia, looking around her.

"Here we are. I'm parched," said Lady-Bird, pointing to a hole in the wall with a small cluster of tables and chairs gathered in front of it. Not far off there was a shifty goat-face man in a leather jacket, tearing strips off a piece of paper and chewing them violently. He was talking into a tin can that was connected to a piece of string.

"Hester and I used to do that!" Cecilia said, recognising the instrument, and for a passing moment feeling like she recognised the goat-faced man; had she seen him before? Maybe on the way to the Ride or Sigh competition.

"What, talk on the line?" asked Luke.

"Yeah," Cecilia said.

A voice jumped out at them from a hole in the wall.

"What'll it be then, chaps?" The voice belonged to a rabbit-face in a red bow tie.

Then another rabbit-face with a bow tied around her ear said: "Liquorice tea? Hot or cold?" The rabbit-faced duo spoke very quickly.

Cecilia noticed that the two heads shared only one body.

"I'll have mine cold," said Luke. "Cecilia?"

"Yes, I'll have the same please."

"And I'll have mine hot," said Lady-Bird.

"Better for the vocal chords, I suspect, Miss Lady-Bird," said the rabbit-face in the bow tie, throwing her a knowing wink.

"Quite right, Robert," said Lady-Bird.

"Have a seat, we'll bring them over when they're ready."

"Thank you, Jennifer... Robert."

"Our pleasure," they chimed.

Cecilia, Luke and Lady-Bird walked over to a little round table with a tessellated diamond design on its top. They sat down and the goat-face on the line had become so animated it was difficult to ignore him. Robert and Jennifer brought the drinks over and put them down on the table. As Lady-Bird felt in her pockets for some buttons, the two rabbit-faces said in unison, "Please, Miss, they're on the house."

Luke raised his eyebrows at Cecilia and sipped his drink.

The three of them said thank you and Cecilia took a sip of the clean, refreshing liquid. Lady-Bird sat peacefully and after scanning the area, she removed her goggle glasses, set them gently on the table, untied her headscarf and leant back in her chair.

"You know," she said, "you guys remind me of Kuffi and me when we were younger. He was my best friend. Before Jacques d'Or came into our lives and ruined it all."

Lady-Bird looked into Cecilia's eyes.

"I guess I was frightened of Jacques d'Or. He had so much power and it just kept growing." Lady-Bird bowed her head for a moment then continued. "But now I know it's no use counting your friends if the ones you have can't count on you. I let Kuffi down big-time."

"At least you're trying to make it up to him now," said Cecilia.

"I just hope it's not too late." Lady-Bird blew on her liquorice tea and sipped it with her beak.

Her expression changed when the goat-face man in the corner started shouting angrily, "Just hurry up! We don't have long." He flung the tin receiver on the ground and kicked it about in the dirt. Then he turned to Lady-Bird, Cecilia and Luke.

"I wouldn't fancy being the poor chap on the other side," whispered Lady-Bird.

"What are you looking at?" the goat-face shouted.

They tried to ignore him but he continued shouting. "Hey, wait a minute," he said, pointing at Lady-Bird. "Don't I know you?"

He started towards them.

"I don't think so," said Lady-Bird, rising out of her seat and gathering herself. Cecilia quickly handed Lady-Bird the goggle glasses she had taken off and thrust her scarf towards her, but it was too late.

"Yeah, you're that bird that sings. Lady-Bird. That's the one!" he was standing at their table now, looming over them. Cecilia felt very uncomfortable. She looked at Luke, who was beginning to rise out of his chair; Cecilia rested her hand on his arm. Lady-Bird called over for help but Robert and Jennifer appeared to be frozen to the spot with fear. Cecilia searched the red tunnel in both directions but there was no one else about.

"You're coming with me!" growled the goat-face.

"Hey, get off her!" screamed Cecilia at the top of her lungs.

"Don't you dare!" said Luke, lowering his head and threatening him with his antlers.

"Ha ha ha!" mocked the goat-face. "And what do you think you're going to do with those baby stumps? Give me a head massage? I don't think so!" he said, wrenching Lady-Bird up and out of her seat.

"Let go of me!" cried Lady-Bird.

The goat-face spat some chewed-up paper on the ground and started waffling on about how he'd been keeping an eye on Cecilia and Luke for a while. "We knew you were up to something," he said. "But you were worth the wait, cos now you've given us Lady-Bird, and Jacques d'Or will see we are on his side!"

"We?" said Luke. "Us?"

"Heya, Lukey," called a voice from behind all the commotion.

"Ella Bear. Get back, this guy is dangerous."

"I know," she said. "I like to call him Garry Goat-face... Killer!" She laughed. "He's a friend of mine. We're working together—you could say we're besties. Right, Garry? Who do you think was on the other end of the line? Thank goodness for that hole in the wall, otherwise I'd have had to go all the way round. Anyway, like I said last time I bumped into you, Lukey Bear, you owe me... now you're all paid up. Come on, Garry, and bring Lady-Bird with you. He'll be thrilled to have her back. He doesn't like it when others take what belongs to him!"

"No, Ella Bear, wait!"

"For what?" she said. "I've got what I came for. Garry and I make a great team, don't cha' fink?"

Ella Bear wasn't a bear cub at all, just a cute bear with a very good cover-up act!

"Come on, Garry!" she shouted as she began to walk off. "Jacques d'Or will be waiting for us with a very tidy sum!"

"You work for Jacques d'Or?"

"Who else?" Ella Bear called out without looking back.

Garry started dragging Lady-Bird off with him and Cecilia yanked at his jacket, but he was much stronger than her and flung her to the ground. Luke was hurt and enraged. He backed off to get a run up at Garry, then charged forward, but the goat-face jumped out of the way and Luke dived headfirst into the tunnel wall.

"Amateur," Garry sneered.

Cecilia grabbed hold of Garry's arm but Lady-Bird pleaded with her to stop.

"Leave it, Cecilia, you might get hurt."

"What? No, Lady-Bird!"

"It's OK. Stick together, you'll be fine." She turned to the goat-face. "I don't want any more trouble. I'll come but on my own terms!"

"But where is he taking you?" cried Cecilia.

"Back to the Nest, I suspect?"

"Yep, Jacques d'Or will be very pleased with me for escorting you back. Maybe he'll even give me a permanent job!" said Garry the goat-face in a very loud voice.

"NO! Nooooo!" screamed Cecilia, grabbing at his coat again. "I won't let you."

"Cecilia, it's OK. Just stick together and do what we talked about and it'll be OK."

Cecilia was furious and unrelenting. She tugged at Garry's coat a third time and he snapped. He'd finally had enough. Garry swung his head round and butted her in the forehead. Cecilia hurtled to the ground.

"I'm coming with you!" Cecilia shouted after them.

"Cecilia," called Lady-Bird as Garry dragged her along,

"you need to wait here for Luke to come round or he won't know what's happened."

Cecilia, filled with frustration, cupped her head in her hands, rubbed her face furiously and let out a stifled scream. Not Lady-Bird too, she thought.

Luke sat up and rubbed his head, which was wet with blood. "What's going on?"

"Ella Bear and Garry, they've taken Lady-Bird back to the Nest." She sobbed.

"Hang on, Cecilia. Isn't that where we need her to be anyway?"

22

Black Forest

Cecilia plonked herself down in her chair. "What now?" she asked.

"I guess we have to keep on with the plan."

"But how will we find Mr Sparks without Lady-Bird?"

"I think Lady-Bird said something about it being close to the Nest. I feel like I've passed it before when I had to hide out in the Black Forest."

Luke noticed that Robert and Jennifer appeared to be returning to their usual selves after apparently being frozen to the spot with fear amid all the commotion.

"Cecilia, I think we should get a move on before they start asking questions."

Cecilia looked about at the scattered chairs and tables and spilt drinks and over to the line which was off the hook.

"OK, let's go." Suddenly she felt very guilty. What if Garry came looking for them, she thought.

"We will head into the Black Forest for now. At least we can hide there while we work out what to do once we get to Mr Sparks," said Luke.

Cecilia and Luke were tired. They walked along in silence. Luke's head was still bleeding but not too badly. Cecilia stopped him, and took his trousers out of her rucksack and paused to tie them around his head in a makeshift bandage.

"That'll do for now," Cecilia said, tucking the ends in.

"Thanks," said Luke.

As they continued to walk the tunnel sloped down into a sea of tall, thin shadows.

"There it is!" Luke whispered loudly as the Black Forest came into view. They'd been so close when Lady-Bird got taken away, thought Cecilia. Luke stared into the rows and rows of trees in front of them. Cecilia watched him walk into them as she paused to take in such a magnificent sight. Luke was inspecting the long dark tree trunks. He looked dwarfed standing amongst them when Cecilia saw a ghostly figure dodging through the dark.

"I think we've got company..." she said, searching the undergrowth for the figure. "Luke?"

Cecilia turned back and Luke was gone.

"Luke!" she called timidly at first, her eyes darting about the space. "Luke, this isn't funny!" Her breathing began to race, her heart pounding in her chest. She grabbed her head in both her hands and, raising her voice to a deafening roar, screamed: "Luke! LUKE! LUUUUUUUUUUUKE!"

She paused a moment, her body rocking on the spot. "No, no, no, no, no..." she muttered under her breath, shaking her head. "No, this can't be happening."

A voice crept out of the looming trees. "That's an awful racket you're making for such a little girl!" it goaded. "Are you going to cry for me?" it said, rattling through the undergrowth and into her ears.

Cecilia's skin crawled and although she was fearful, she was entirely defiant. She looked down the avenues of black trees, trying to locate the hidden voice.

"Weep!" the voice demanded, ricocheting off the deep bowels of the tunnels.

"WEEP!" it shouted, demonic and cold. She saw the ghostly figure again, flickering through the undergrowth, and she knew now it was Jacques d'Or. She strained her ears to listen, poised like a wild creature.

"I must say you've done well to get this far, Cecilia. I didn't make it easy; but then if it were easy it would be boring, wouldn't it?" came the voice of Jacques d'Or, who was still hidden in the trees. It seemed to have a faint smile held within it. It wasn't mocking, more enjoying its own sound, its own existence: arrogant and wise all at once. Proud.

"I know who you are, Jacques d'Or!" shouted Cecilia.

A slow clap shivered through the overhanging boughs.

"What do you want, a prize?"

Cecilia tried to stay unruffled but her voice quivered ever so slightly in her throat, giving her away. "How do you know my name?" She straightened herself up, trying to control the rage spilling into her body and flooding her brain.

"Tell me, Cecilia, how do you know when you are at the end of something? If something's over? How do you know when you've reached the end of the line?"

Cecilia stood quietly, thinking about what the voice was trying to say, as she searched for the right words to reply.

"When you can't go any further?" she replied.

"Close, try again."

"I don't have to answer your stupid questions," she shouted.

"Well, it might buy you a bit more time to live if you do!" taunted Jacques d'Or.

Cecilia hesitated. The voice continued, "I mean, if you're still alive, it can't be over yet, can it? So, when is something finished?"

"When you've got nothing left and no where else to go." Cecilia willed Luke to come back with all her heart but she knew that Jacques d'Or must've got him too.

"Bingo! And it looks as though a little someone may have reached the finish line, but sadly she's lost!"

Thoughts began to dash about Cecilia's head but she stood rooted to the spot.

"You see, Cecilia, there's nowhere else to go and your friends can't help you now. We've been following you and we know about your nasty little plan to overthrow the Corvus Community. So we think we will dispose of you before you cause any more mischief. You should've known better. I have eyes in the shadows. I am everywhere!"

Cecilia winced as his voice boomed out of the trees and bounced off the darkness above.

"I just wondered if you realised your time is up or if you still thought you had a chance?"

"I..." Cecilia paused. "What have you done with my friends?" she said, raising her voice.

"Well, we do like to jump to conclusions, don't we, Cecilia!" Jacques d'Or was in full swing now. "But you would be right. Like so many other damned creatures I do happen to have them in my possession. Such a splendid collection, and that stag-face boy, let him mature a bit and he'll make a glorious wall feature!" Jacques d'Or was having a right good time now. She could tell by the way he stretched his words and curled the ends of his sentences.

"You owe me," he said sharply.

"What for?" she replied incredulously.

"For all the trouble you've caused, for all the rumours that you've started to spread, for the hope that you were planning to plant into the hearts of these poor innocent dwellers." Then in a fit of rage he screamed like a banshee: "HOW DARE YOU TAKE MY LADY-BIRD!"

"She's not yours! Lady-Bird isn't a possession, she belongs to herself!" Cecilia shouted back as she saw him rise up into the canopy a few rows ahead.

"Be quiet! You owe me. I'll have all your tears, every last drop. Until you are shrivelled up and dried out from crying a river to fill our lake with your lifetime!"

Cecilia thought he was being a bit dramatic, and it occurred to her that maybe if she hit the right nerve, she might get him to at least reveal some of the details about her friends. In all the movies she'd ever seen, villains simply can't help themselves. It's part of how they get revenge: by making their victim suffer as they reveal the truth, believing that they will have the last word as they hold their victim in their evil clutches. Anyway, besides her rucksack, she really didn't have much to lose any more, and if there was any way she could find one last chance to save her friends and get home, it was worth a shot.

"Why are you hiding from me?" she called up into the boughs of the trees, taking small, quiet steps towards his last landing spot. "Come out and face me, or are you afraid?"

As she worked her way into the forest and it became brighter, fireflies filled the air. Jacques d'Or swooped down from his perch and stood in front of her, beaming. He pulled a mirror from his waistcoat and rearranged his feathers, smoothing out some ruffled tufts on his crown.

"Jacques d'Or," she said. "Pleased to finally meet you."

"I wish I shared your sentiment but you really are a thorn in my side at the moment," he said spitefully.

"Nice mirror," she remarked.

"Isn't it just?" he said, snapping it shut and twitching with rage.

There was a flapping as he rose up storming into the trees. They rustled and bent under the weight of such a large bird.

"Now all that's left is to decide what to do with you... It seems you're more trouble than your tears are worth. So, I could push you into the pits of the doldrums and let a gas explosion blast you to smithereens. Or what about taking you out to the Black of Beyond and leaving you lost in the dark? No, that won't do; you might somehow find your way back. I know! I'll just throw you in the Deep at the end of the Black Forest instead. I am pretty sure no one would miss you!"

"The Deep?" Cecilia was puzzled. She remembered Jasper saying something about the Deep when she was inspecting a jar of his.

"The Deep... The black hole of no return?" Jacques d'Or sounded irritated. "No one who enters the Deep comes back because it goes nowhere!"

Cecilia steadied herself. The Deep sounded scary but what if no one ever wanted to come back because whatever was on the other side of it was far better than here... It wouldn't be impossible, she thought. Cecilia couldn't really imagine nothingness. An infinite deepness, yes, or a portal to elsewhere seemed more reasonable. She remembered from watching TV that black holes usually took you somewhere, and what she'd learnt from being in the tunnels so far was that every tunnel led on to another one, so the Deep must go somewhere too, and besides, surely Jasper wouldn't have a jar of it in his cubby if it was seriously harmful?

"Let's spice things up a bit, shall we?" Jacques d'Or blew on a small gold whistle hanging on a chain from his waistcoat pocket.

"It would be a bit of a bore to just push you into the Deep. Let's chase you there first!"

A large dog-face approached and stood under the tree that Jacques d'Or was weighing down. The dog-face had the sad drooping guise of a boxer dog but he also looked mean. Very mean.

"Perfect!" said Jacques d'Or. "Cecilia, meet Hunter. Hunter, meet Cecilia. Now that you've met we'd better crack on. Hunter, you are to chase Cecilia into the Deep. Got it?"

Hunter turned slowly and looked up into the trees and then back at Cecilia. He seemed tired and weary but agreed with a nod of his head.

Jacques d'Or hopped down to the ground.

"Now, Cecilia, I'm not an unreasonable chap so I'll give you a head start."

"But I—" She made to speak but Jacques d'Or interrupted her.

"I'm afraid the time for discussion is over. Twenty seconds on the clock! Hunter, on all fours now," Jacques d'Or commanded. Hunter let out a deep, low grunt and stood staring at Jacques d'Or. "Disobedience won't be tolerated now, will it, hmm?" Jacques d'Or toyed with the small gold whistle dangling from the chain on his waistcoat. "Hmm?" he goaded. "On all fours, now, there's the sport, it's much more fun this way."

Hunter settled into a moment of utter humiliation as he got on his furry hands and knees.

"Fabulous. Ready, Cecilia? On your marks... Get set..."

Cecilia had hardly a moment to think and had no idea where to go.

"GO! Run, run for your life!" Jacques d'Or shouted, a cackling laugh clinging onto the end of his words before he began counting.

"**One...**" Cecilia ran through the darkest patches of the trees, running as fast as she could into the cloak of their shadowy boughs.

"**Two...**" She stopped and looked up, wondering if she should climb one and try to hide in the branches, but she knew eventually Hunter would sniff her out or Jacques d'Or would swoop in and spot her from above.

"**Three... Four... Five...**"
She knew she had to keep moving so she kept running, not knowing where she was going or if she would find a place of safety. Then she had an idea.

"**Six... Seven...**"
She leant up against the trees, her mind racing. The Deep—she would look for the black hole. It would be better to choose to jump in instead...

"**Eight...** Oh, this is getting exciting!" Jacques d'Or's voice was getting audibly quieter as she moved further away from him but still she could hear the shrill of excitement in it.

"Nine... Ten... Eleven..."

Sweat had formed on her brow. And she ran, scratching her arms and legs on the branches, dodging in all directions to try to buy some extra time. If she could give Hunter a jagged trail, it might take him longer to find her.

"Twelve... Thirteen... Fourteen... Fifteen..."

And then she spotted it, not far off. Stunning and magical, the Deep that Jacques d'Or had condemned her to was exactly like the substance Jasper had in the jar at his cubby. A small blossoming tree hung over it, a pool of silvery liquid gel. The Deep looked like a rip in the ground, morphing and undulating like liquid metal. She could've cried but she refused to, knowing that was what Jacques d'Or wanted. His voice grew fainter as she sped further and further away from it. But she knew soon it would be upon her once again if she didn't keep going. Cecilia could still hear him faintly talking to himself about how wonderful he was and all the changes he had made to the tunnels to improve them and how she'd almost ruined everything. Cecilia ran towards the pool of liquid. She ran for her life. She strained her ears to listen; she could really use Jasper's ear horn now.

"Sixteen... Seventeen... Eighteen..."

Panting, she pushed on, running faster than she had ever run. She shot out of the silhouetted trees with all her might and with nothing but her will and her legs to carry her.

"Nineteen... Twenty... Ready or not, here we c-o-m-e!" cried the far-off voice of Jacques d'Or. It was bordering on the edge of a joyful squeal.

"Release the HUNTER!" echoed through the menacing treetops.

Although Cecilia wasn't there to witness it, Hunter looked at Jacques d'Or with a disappointed grimace and shook his head. A flush of embarrassment passed over his brow. He sighed and began to move off, shuffling along on the ground. Jacques d'Or snapped a branch off a nearby tree and tossed it in the air, shouting "Fetch" in a patronising voice. "There's a good boy, now off you trot. She's getting away!"

Cecilia paused by the edge of the trees at an opening where the Deep was located. She crept over to the single blossoming tree and a flurry of soft pink and white petals floated by her as she peered into the small pool over which it hung. The tree was a winter-blossoming cherry tree. She knew because it was her mum's favourite and there was one at the end of their road back home. When in bloom its petals would float into the air like snow. She focused her eyes on the pool. Mum, she thought. "Home," she whispered to herself as she saw her own face reflected in the liquid.

Is this the Deep? she wondered. Surely not, it's no bigger than my living room and it doesn't seem all that scary. She'd expected something more like the Grand Canyon but there it was: a small, calm, reflective pool. Granted, she couldn't see beyond the surface but it had a tranquillity about it. Cecilia stood a few feet from the edge and watched as it morphed before her, lighting up the blossom on the tree with its mirrored surface and absorbing the blossom that fell onto it.

She was close to getting into the Deep when fear tapped her on the shoulder, an uninvited foe, and just to top things off it had brought its best mate—doubt. She stood motionless. She tried to bat the bad thoughts away but they pushed in. What if there's something in there? Or worse still, what if there's nothing, nothing at all? But she had to do it; there was no where else to go. Cecilia could hear Jacques d'Or's voice dancing closer. He was unhinged! What was he going to do to Kuffi, Luke and Lady-Bird? She knew that this was her only chance to get away. She imagined her friends trapped and crying for eternity; she owed it to them and to herself. Jacques d'Or was chattering away as he grew nearer, so at least she knew where he was, but it also meant Hunter wouldn't be far either. Cecilia decided in that moment that there was no time for fear and certainly no room for doubt. She sucked up a long breath and backed away from the edge a little so she could get a run-up and with arms outstretched she launched at the pool in front of her and disappeared into the Deep.

23

The Deep

The first thing Cecilia noticed was that she was cold. There were no two ways about it: she was freezing. She appeared to be moving through a glossy expanse of silvery liquid, an oily slick to nowhere, as far as she could tell. Although she could feel her body moving through the substance, Cecilia found it hard to actually move the parts of her body; she was stuck in the position she had made on entry. She kept her breath held and though things were blurry, she could make out flecks of silver and blue, like glitter rushing past her. Cecilia wondered if Hunter had managed to sniff her out, and if he had, if he'd be forced to follow her? Hopefully, if they did trace her to the Deep, Jacques d'Or would give up and leave her to her fate. She strained her neck to look behind her and as she did, she almost let out a scream: a giant version of Jacques d'Or was saying something, but it was muffled, like when she was underwater in the bath and her mum came in, and she could almost hear her but it was all smudged. Had Cecilia moved at all? He looked so close. She decided to try to swim. As she did she felt a resistance to push against, a bit like moving through jelly, but it wasn't sticky. She knew she didn't have long until she would need to breathe, so she tried to keep swimming—if you could call it swimming.

She heard a clicking sound echoing about her and wondered what it was. It was a creaking pattern that made the gelatinous substance wobble. Her lungs were starting to pull on her chest for air. What would happen if she did just try to breathe in? Cecilia began to feel weak and light headed when there came a forceful tug on her leg, and she was yanked deep, deep down as it all went black.

When Cecilia came to she was lying on a bed of dry moss, looking up at a ceiling bedecked with what looked like tiny stars. She wasn't cold any more and although she could feel the atmosphere was damp, she felt herself to be quite dry at least. She could see her rucksack hung up over the wall and she sat upright, climbed off the mossy bed and went over to check her belongings were still there. She held the marble in her hand for a moment, feeling relief, then put it back. This didn't look like the work of Jacques d'Or: he wouldn't hang her rucksack up for her and she didn't appear to be imprisoned. As she searched the room, Cecilia discovered that she was standing in a small, glittering cave. A serene sound came to her, like a whale or a dolphin call. She didn't know the language of the sounds that it spoke, but somehow she understood its meaning and recognised it as the sound that had come to her through the Deep.

"The substance on the walls—it's a type of bioluminescence... living light." The words of the soft, smooth voice were being transmitted directly into her head.

"Oh," said Cecilia out loud. She wasn't feeling very well. Whoever it was standing in the doorway was just outside of view.

"My name is Doltha and I belong to a small community of Divers who live here. I have some broth for you, it should help with the decompression sickness you might be feeling. Here you are." From the shadows she held the bowl out. "It should warm you up too. I thought you might be hungry."

Doltha stepped forward to reveal a dorsal fin, flippers, a tail, and arms and legs, all covered in a smooth pinkish complexion. Her eyes were quite human, but almost entirely black. Cecilia had to save herself from gasping. She was quite beautiful.

Doltha placed the small black wooden bowl in Cecilia's hands. "Try some," she said encouragingly.

Cecilia brought the bowl up to her lips and instantly felt at ease. She sipped it slowly. It was delicious: it tasted like a concoction of mushrooms and raw peas and clams;

it was warm and soothing like Doltha's voice. Her eyes were kind, and as Cecilia looked into them, they seemed to invite her trust.

"You've been through quite a lot. It's been a long time since anyone has entered the Deep, and usually they've been pushed or thrown in to be disposed of, but it's been a very long time since someone actually had the courage to choose to face it themselves. You did well."

"I didn't know what else to do." Cecilia sat down on the moss-covered bed, looking sadly into her bowl.

"You trusted yourself and your instincts. You did the right thing and stayed true to yourself, even if it was hard. The Deep is only as boundless as you let it be," said Doltha.

"Doltha, if I may... where am I?" asked Cecilia.

"Ah ha," she said. "Think of the Deep as a window. You've done the hardest part; you are now on the other side of that window."

"Oh." Cecilia left a long pause. "Doltha, it's all gone terribly wrong. You don't want me here, I'm nothing but trouble." Cecilia held back from crying; she wasn't sure what Doltha would make of it.

"I had to leave my friends," Cecilia continued. "But what will come of them? I have to get back to the Black Forest and get them out of the Nest. I have to help them, Doltha, please? I can't stay here and do nothing!" Cecilia stood up.

"Drink some more broth, it will make you feel better," said Doltha.

Cecilia sat back down and drank the rest of the broth.

"I sense that you don't believe what's happening to you."

"Sometimes I have moments when I know where I am and what's going on, but then everything changes again. It's a lot to take in. I just want to go home."

"Until you accept your situation and the nature of the environment that you find yourself to be existing in..."

"Oh, sorry, my name is Cecilia..."

"...Cecilia," Doltha continued, "then you can not expect to change it. I think you need to accept the circumstances you have found yourself in so that you can move forwards. We can help you do that and help find your friends but first we will need to discuss what action to take."

Doltha looked at Cecilia knowingly and picked up the empty bowl. "I'll be back to get you shortly. There is a deepsuit hanging up on the wall for you. It will keep you warm and dry. I'll leave you a little while to get changed and inform Gaia that you are awake." With that, Doltha left.

Cecilia did as she was told and got changed into the deepsuit. It was fitted her well. It was chocolate brown and covered in a soft fuzz. She folded up her dress and went to her bag to try to stuff it in alongside her own clothes and Luke's hoody. Cecilia reached into her coat pocket and retrieved the marble once more; this time she took it out and held it in her palm. Cecilia examined the marble closely. She wondered where it came from and what its real purpose might be. After all, something had changed when they'd held it up to Polaris. Did it belong here? Or was it just a stupid piece of glass? She felt frustrated and ashamed. She thought about it and remembered that actually it was the thing that had got her into all this trouble in the first place. She felt weighed down by it and a small flame of anger flared up inside her. "It doesn't mean anything. It's pointless and heavy. It's just a bit of old tat!" She groaned with frustrated anguish. "This is a piece of rubbish," she growled, realising that nothing could ever replace what she had lost. She became rigid and tense and bursting into a fit of absolute rage, she lobbed the marble at the wall in front of her with all her might and all her fury.

In the instant that she hurled it, she came back to her senses with a tinge of regret. She waited to hear the shattering sound as the glassy orb broke into thousands of pieces—her eyes clenched shut, shoulders hunched. But no sound came. She dropped her shoulders and opened one eye, then the other and saw that the marble sphere had landed up on a ledge where it rolled around in circles, catching the light of the lamp next to it. A kaleidoscope of colours burst from it and the bioluminescent particles on the walls bounced it back all around her in thin shafts of light—like tiny lasers. The marble began to circle round faster and wider. Cecilia's stood in awe as the orb spun off the ledge and into the air, spinning rapidly on an invisible axis.

She was astonished. It looked like a tiny star glowing from within and projecting its light and warmth. Cecilia shaded her eyes, squinting at the marble as it burned brighter and brighter. She let out a huge sigh that turned to white puffs like clouds passing around the sphere. It was like a miniature weather system in the room. The mood changed as the sphere began to move around the room erratically, the clouds casting shadows with small bursts of rain erupting. Cecilia held her hands out to catch the raindrops and laughed. The laughter caused bright pulses of warmth to surge from the orb. Cecilia approached the marble sphere and blew softly on the clouds and they moved, her breath turning to a light breeze that picked up and murmured around the room. It was incredible. She made to touch the marble sphere—but it was hot, almost too hot to touch.

Her fascination was interrupted by the sound of Doltha's voice. "Ah, excuse me, Cecilia, but there's someone I'd like you to meet."

Doltha smiled, looking at the marble sphere.

"Cecilia, meet Gaia." Eight tentacles and a bulbous head rested above a body of hands and legs, feet and arms. An octopus-face stood proudly before Cecilia, tendrils outstretched in the same way Hester might draw a picture of the sun. She was a deepish red colour. Cecilia was overwhelmed.

"Hello, Gaia, pleased to meet you." She held out her hand, not knowing where to look or what limb to shake.

"Tentacle or hand? Which will it be?" Gaia jested.

"Tentacle?" Cecilia replied.

"Pick a number."

"Err, three."

And they both giggled at each another as Gaia extended her third tentacle and shook Cecilia's hand; it was quite sticky and a little bit slimy. While she was holding Cecilia's hand in her tentacle, Gaia turned to Doltha and smiled. "I like this one, she can stay." She looked back at Cecilia and winked.

"Now then," said Gaia. "Looks like someone's stumbled onto something rather special!" Gaia extended a tentacle towards the spinning marble. Cecilia got the feeling that Gaia was quite important.

"Have you figured out what it is yet?" she asked Cecilia.

"I thought it was a marble but obviously I was wrong."

"We call it an elemental sphere and it's been missing for quite some time. This elemental sphere belongs to a whole network actually, but without one, the chain is broken and the system becomes defunct, then none of them work. So I think we need to get this back where it belongs," said Gaia.

"Do you mean Polaris?"

"She doesn't miss a beat, does she?" said Gaia, nudging Doltha.

"Yes, you're spot on," Gaia said in answer to her question.

"Will that mean Mr Sparks can go back to the lake?"

"Ah, Mr Sparks, that poor fellow has been through an awful lot. Yes, exactly that," said Gaia. "It looks as though you were sent here to set us straight, Cecilia." Gaia strolled over to Cecilia and put a hand gently on her shoulder.

"I don't suppose it's going to be easy but then I suspect that you're no stranger to a bit of a challenge. Get some rest and we will call a meeting with the Diving Council to work out what we should do next." Gaia extended a tentacle towards the elemental sphere but stopped herself and instead turned back towards Cecilia.

"May I? It does belong to you, after all," she said.

"Of course." Cecilia hung her head a moment; it felt like she was giving away her last piece of home, but she realised the elemental sphere wasn't just a piece of bric-a-brac any more—it was part of a complex and difficult system that might change the lives of all the dwellers, and hopefully her own. She reached her hand towards the elemental sphere. It was warm. Cecilia had to tug at it quite hard to get a hold on it, but once it was free it began to cool down and its light faded. She handed it to Gaia.

"Thank you, Cecilia," said Gaia, throwing her another wink.

24

Hexagon Hall

Cecilia could hear Doltha's voice inside her head, telling her that the Diving Council members were ready to meet her and that she should join them in the Hexagon Hall.

"Follow my voice," Doltha said softly. "Are you ready?"

"Yes," said Cecilia, approaching the door in a sort of trance.

"Excellent. Now, as you leave your room, turn left and walk straight along the corridor. You will pass two doors one each side. When you get to the end of the passage, climb the staircase directly in front of you. Call on me when you get to the top and I will meet you there, outside Hexagon Hall. Is that clear?"

Cecilia had already begun the journey. "Thank you, Doltha, I'll find my way."

"Call me if you need me," Doltha replied.

Cecilia walked along the passage, passing the doors Doltha had mentioned, and took the stairs to a landing where a window looked out into the Deep. There was no glass as such, just a bubble made of the silvery substance she had found herself stuck in. Cecilia climbed the rest of the stairs where she waited for Doltha to come out. She stood in a small atrium covered in moss and gemstones and hand-painted tiles that seemed to depict the history of the tunnels, the dwellers and the Divers.

Doltha popped her head around a small wooden door and met her in the middle of the small space.

"Did you call? I didn't hear you."

"I just needed a moment to prepare to meet everyone," said Cecilia, just shy of a whisper.

"Everyone is very excited to meet you," Doltha said.

Cecilia's nervousness felt like it had transformed into hundreds of creepy-crawlies inside her and they were making her hands tremble. "It's OK, they don't bite," said Doltha as she turned to lead the way. Cecilia noticed that when Doltha smiled her eyes made two dark crescents.

Doltha took Cecilia's hand in hers and pushed open the door to the Hexagon Hall.

"Awesome" was the only word to describe the six-sided room that looked very much like a chapel. The roof was painted with an elaborate frieze that resembled a bright star with lots of other scenes of the dwellers connected to it. There were four more members of the Diving Council sitting around a large limestone hexagonal slab, which had a separate gemstone plinth located a few feet away from it. The members of the Diving Council were all smiling at Cecilia, and one of them rose to his feet and thrust his hand in Cecilia's direction eagerly.

"Hi, Cecilia, pleased to meet you. I'm Owen." Owen was a seal-face with big shiny eyes right out of a cartoon; he was only a pup.

Cecilia sat down in an unoccupied seat next to Doltha. "Hi," she whispered back.

Cecilia noticed that the elemental sphere—her marble—was stationed at the centre of the table on a mossy cushion. The cushion was glowing with tiny blue flecks all around it, and she felt a twinge of excitement surge through her upon seeing it again. It was amazing how quickly her marble had taken on a whole new status! It meant so much more than she could have ever imagined. It was something really special to the dwellers and their society.

Gaia stood up and raised all of her tentacles in the air to signify that the meeting was officially beginning. When there was silence Gaia held up a glassy spear with a crystal handgrip. Each of the members of the council followed suit until all the spears were held in the air. With a swift flick up and down, Gaia's spear lit up bright blue. Each of the members of the council took it in turns to hold up their spears and copied the action until the room turned blue.

"We're ready to proceed in delivering the plan we have devised," said a cat-face, letting out a gentle purr as she spoke.

"That's Jestyna," Doltha whispered into Cecilia's brain. Jestyna was sleek and black and she looked pretty strong. Cecilia suspected she could pose quite a threat to the Corvus Community.

"There are two essential aims of the mission," Jestyna continued. "To release Mr Sparks back into the lake, and to reinstall the elemental sphere."

Jestyna sat down, and a rather handsome wolf-face chap took over.

"Our main concerns are the safety of Mr Sparks when he is in transition to the lake and if there will be enough water to hold him when he arrives."

"Do we have a plan if this were not the case?" asked Gaia with a very serious expression on her face.

"Not exactly," said the wolf-face, sitting back down.

"Thank you, Adriene. Are there any suggestions for how we can secure enough water for Mr Sparks if he is returned safely to the lake?"

Cecilia feebly raised her hand.

"Yes, Cecilia, please stand. What are your thoughts?" Gaia asked.

"It's a long shot but could we not request that the dwellers lend their tears one last time while we return the elemental sphere to its rightful place?" She quickly sat back down when she had finished and Doltha patted her proudly on the back.

There was some mumbling and conferring among the council before Gaia spoke again.

"It is not a bad idea; it would take some rallying around. But we shan't rule it out."

"What if we transferred him to the Deep?" suggested Owen.

"No, that won't work," said the final member of the council left to speak. He had been standing in the shadows behind Owen and now Cecilia could see why: he was a shark-face and although he didn't come across as scary, he looked very fierce.

"Don't be alarmed by Rory," Doltha whispered to Cecilia. "He's a great guy; very, very smart and extremely fast!"

"Mr Sparks needs to be returned to the lake. Who knows what the Deep would do to him. He could be lost for eternity!" said Rory.

"Oh dear," said Cecilia, hardly making a sound.

"Plus, we don't know how damaged he will be. Jacques d'Or has used Mr Sparks as a pure source of light in and of himself by hooking up his thousands of tentacles to silicon tubes that span the entire network of tunnels for a very long time now." Rory started to circle the hexagonal table as he spoke.

"For those members of our party who are new to this discussion, those miles and miles of tubes that keep the tunnels bright, the energy that powers them—that's Mr Sparks. His tentacles are encased in tubes of saline fluid. That's why there's such a great need for regular lamentation; the salty tears lubricate the tubes, and without it Mr Sparks would dry up and die.

"That is until now. The elemental sphere has been returned and we just have to put it back where it belongs to restore harmony to the tunnels. This alone will ensure the safe return of Mr Sparks back where he belongs.

"It looks like Cecilia's backup plan might be our best hope if something goes wrong. But why would the dwellers listen to us? We will be strangers to them who've just turned up out of the Deep from nowhere."

Cecilia raised her hand with a little bit more confidence this time.

"Well, they might not listen to us but they will definitely listen to Madame Midnight, Kuffi and Lady-Bird. As far as I can tell they're some of the most well-known and well-respected dwellers in the tunnels but at the moment they're being held captive by Jacques d'Or. If we set them free, then they will help us gather all the dwellers together to stand united against Jacques d'Or and the Corvus Community, and if Lady-Bird sings a song by the lake, we'll have everyone one in tears in no time—but hopefully, tears of joy!"

"All in favour, say aye!" called Gaia and with that all the members of the Diving Council raised their spears and the room flashed electric blue and returned to how it was before.

Cecilia raised her hand one more time.

"Yes, Cecilia, you have something more to say?" Gaia asked.

Cecilia stood up. "No, actually, I just wanted to say thank you." And she sat back down.

"Cecilia, we have been waiting for an opportunity like this one for such a long time. The Corvus Community drove the Divers out of the tunnels. You see, bird-faces aren't too keen on cats or canines and most of what's left of that species are locked away in the egg cells at the Nest, or kept on leashes as servants. A few of them found their way over to us through the Deep where they are safe and cared for, but not many. This is our chance to set it right and restore harmony."

Cecilia looked at the etchings on the wall as Gaia went through the details of the plan. They depicted a time when everyone looked happy and peaceful together.

Gaia raised her spear. "In summary then, everyone, prepare yourselves and gather your things. We will meet shortly at the main entrance to the Deep, where we will start our mission to restore the tunnels to their former glory and help our new friend save her friends. Hopefully it won't all end in tears, but if there's not enough water for Mr Sparks it may have to, and we will be ready."

Doltha walked Cecilia back to her room and helped her to pack up her belongings, what little there were. After Doltha had left to go and prepare herself, Cecilia sat down to eat a Cherry Drop. Getting it out of its wrapper was tough. It was really gooey and sticky from being in the Deep. She popped it in her mouth and sucked the sticky off—once the outer tacky layer had gone, it tasted just like any other Cherry Drop: delicious! While she sat there with the sweetie rolling around her mouth, she worried about going into the Deep again and hoped this was the last time she'd ever have to do it.

25

The Other Side of Fear

When the signal sounded, it was a gentle, low-pitched drone a bit like a French horn, and a soothing way to wake Cecilia from her mossy bed where she must have fallen asleep. She collected her rucksack and put it on her back, fastening it tight to her shoulders. She was still wearing her deepsuit from earlier, so she was ready to go.

The Divers assembled by the entrance to the Deep. Gaia and Doltha were stirring it with their spears to activate the bioluminescence. Cecilia thought it made it look much more welcoming.

"Are you ready, Cecilia? I'll be diving with you," said Doltha.

"Thanks for all your help. You didn't have to," said Cecilia.

"I believe it's us who should be thanking you. Your arrival may just brighten up the future and the lives of all the dwellers throughout the tunnels." She smiled and Cecilia heard Doltha's voice in her head once more. "Are you scared, Cecilia?"

"A little," Cecilia replied. "I'm not sure what to expect."

"You do, deep, deep down. Just trust yourself and you'll be fine, I promise."

The wolf-face chap looked perturbed. "Is she going in front of us? She'll slow us down, won't she? She looks terrified."

"She's got me, Adriene. We'll be just fine," Doltha said gallantly.

Doltha turned to Cecilia. "We will be submerged for about forty seconds, OK? Maybe less, but trust me. I'll move as fast as I can so hold on tight. Try to keep focused and fight any thoughts that frighten you. And ignore Adriene—he always wants to get to the action first!"

Gaia made the signal; it came from what looked like a large conch, and Doltha and Cecilia eased themselves into the icy cold jelly of the Deep. Doltha's pink skin seemed to glow—she sang out a clicking call and all of a sudden she turned blue. Cecilia's heart was beating like it might punch its way out of her chest and she closed her eyes tight as a coolness rushed over her. Doltha's arms wrapped tightly around her chest and they both took a big breath before plunging into the Deep. A steady rhythm picked up that Cecilia realised was the propulsion of Doltha's head and flipper carrying them at speed through the depth. After Cecilia had counted twenty-six seconds she began to feel the need to take a breath, but she held back with all her might, clamping her eyes shut, trying to stay focused on counting. When she did open her eyes again, Cecilia could just about make out the light of the surface, the small rip she had passed through earlier, growing bigger and bigger the closer they got to it. When they emerged she gasped for breath, exhaling deeply afterwards.

Owen and Rory were already hiding along the trees—they must've been super fast. Then Adriene and Jestyna came up behind them, keeping most of their bodies submerged until they reached the edge by the blossoming tree. The Black Forest was still and quiet, and Cecilia used the trunk of the tree to pull herself out while Doltha pushed her from behind.

Cecilia and Doltha stayed close behind Rory and Owen, who were leading the way up front and looking out for any dangers. The team of Divers travelled through the forest stealthily, trying not to shake the boughs of the trees or otherwise attract any attention.

Cecilia was panting but travelled as quietly as she could.

As they approached the opening where Cecilia and Luke had first met Jacques d'Or, they heard a noise. The group came upon two members of the Corvus Community and held back, Owen holding his furry hand up as a signal to stop. Cecilia knew who they were right away: Julius and

Marvin were sitting counting out buttons, laughing and chatting. They seemed to be guarding a heavy metal door.

"Be careful, Cecilia, there are eyes everywhere. Rory, and Adriene are checking the area, Jestyna will check high up in the shadows first," said Doltha.

"Why them?"

"Well, Jestyna is feline, so she's good at climbing trees and scaling walls and has fantastic night vision. As do Rory and Adriene."

Jestyna got low to the ground and skulked off into the dark. A few moments later there was a screech and a single black feather floated into the clearing. Adriene slipped across the clearing, swiftly removing it from sight.

The three of them worked silently to eliminate the threat posed by the unsuspecting Corvus Community spies dotted around the cavern above the clearing. Rory returned to Doltha and whispered very quietly as if in answer to some silent question: "Fifteen surveillance crows in total. All eyes are out. We should be safe for the time being. We need to get a move on though."

Doltha nodded to Owen, and they watched as the young pup walked bravely up to Julius and Marvin, who were so engrossed in their game, they didn't notice him at first.

"Excuse me," Owen said in the sweetest voice, his huge black eyes already pleading. Julius sprang to his feet, his wings raised instinctively.

"Hold on, Julius. Look at the little thing. He's so cute and he's only little, what harm can he do?" Julius relaxed and sat back in his chair.

"Hey, little one," Marvin said, almost cooing. "What's wrong, are you lost? What you doing down this way, huh?"

"Yes, I'm lost," Owen said, innocently nodding his head.

Julius was taken in too. "Aww, he is cute, Marv!"

"Yeah, bless him. I think he'd even melt Helen's heart, the big ol' raven-face!"

At that moment Owen began barking and clapping loudly. The rest of the Divers rushed to Marvin and Julius who, being so distracted by Owen, had let their guard down. Adriene and Rory leapt on them, silencing them instantly, and they searched for the key to the door Marvin and Julius were supposed to be guarding. They tied their beaks and wings so they couldn't speak or move.

"There's no key!" said Rory, shaking his head.

"What now?" said Doltha, clearly distressed.

Cecilia walked up to the door and turned the handle. It opened, just like that.

Adriene howled with laughter.

"Shhhhh, Adriene! You'll attract too much attention. Now let's scram!" said Doltha.

"Nice one, Cecilia," said Adriene, taking up the lead.

Through the door the tunnel before them was lit with an intense red light, and everyone was silent as they slipped quietly along it. The only sound was the padded footfall of the group running softly through the dust. Adriene the wily wolf-face put his hand up to his ear and they paused as he listened, peering into the dark ahead.

There was a shushing from behind and they fell silent as Rory returned, ushering them to move on.

They travelled along that tunnel for about fifteen minutes at a steady pace, stopping whenever the tunnel turned a corner or went up an incline. At the end, they came to a bright-red NO ENTRY sign. The message was glaringly clear.

"This is it," said Jestyna. "There's no turning back now! Move away..." Jestyna flicked her spear out ready to break the door down, when Cecilia interrupted.

"Just a sec. It's worked for us so far..." she said.

Cecilia turned the handle and the door came open. They all smiled with relief—before they were overcome by the light of a truly dazzling spectacle.

26

Electric Heart

It was true, Mr Sparks was a living thing: a ginormous jellyfish. There he was in all his glory, pulsating in a huge tank in the middle of the room. He was housed in a glass dome about the size of the top of St Paul's Cathedral. Suspended in the tank he was unable to move much, not the way jellyfish normally do, because his tentacles were being used to generate light, feeding through a system of tubes travelling out and away from the tank.

"Wow," whispered Owen as he gazed at the pulsating form of Mr Sparks. The Divers all gathered to stand alongside Doltha and they stared up into the tank at the magnificent Mr Sparks like a group of young children at the edge of a fairground at night. They were spellbound.

Finally someone spoke. "Come on, guys! We had better get to work before someone finds us. We've got no time to lose!"

Doltha approached the tank and pressed her hands up against it and began trying to communicate to Mr Sparks about what was going to happen. Rory told Cecilia and Adriene to position themselves each at one of three big red buttons located around the parameters of Mr Sparks' tank, while Jestyna helped Owen climb to the top of the dome.

A flock of inky figures flooded through the open door and began to raise the alarm, cawing loudly into the generator room.

It was not long before they were surrounded. Cecilia checked to see if the rest of the Divers had taken up their positions. Owen was already inside the tank with Mr Sparks, making his way to the bottom of it to remove the stopper once the buttons had been pressed. Jestyna let out a caterwauling screech and Adriene howled as he might on a full moon. Rory was being attacked by a large crow-face; he thrust his body up and snapped at its leg, giving him just enough time to slam his fist down on his button.

Cecilia waited, she wasn't sure when to press hers; she looked over to Adriene as he continued howling and screeching—he had been wounded by Helen the raven-face but it was hard to tell how badly. He gnashed his jaws and bared his teeth but she was unrelenting, diving at him from above until he managed to grasp her tail feather and knock her off balance, at which point he smashed his hand down on his button with a thump.

Cecilia could see that Mr Sparks was already being sucked downwards to where Owen had removed the stopper. Cecilia knew what she had to do. She drew her hand up, just managing to dodge an overhead attack from an incoming Corvus. Just as she brought it down towards the button, her hand was caught in Hunter's powerful grip. She looked up at him fearfully and he let out a whine as he drew his own hand up and slammed it down on the release button. She smiled at him briefly and ran around to see if anyone else needed her help.

The light began to fade quickly. The chaos stopped as a loud sucking sound reverberated around the generator room. Rory scaled the tank and swam after Owen and Mr Sparks. Some of Mr Sparks' tentacles tore as he was suctioned out of the tank, down the plughole and into the tube. The room went very dark apart from the dying light of the remaining tentacles and a few remaining bioluminescent particles. Cecilia looked at Hunter; he looked down at her with that sad expression and said in a low voice, "The door is still open. Get behind me."

Cecilia could just make out Doltha and a few other Divers being lined up against the tank and strung together. She had no choice but to leave and move forwards through the dark and out of the generator room.

Hunter led her quietly to the door and bade her to leave, when she saw two round eyes flashing beyond it. It was

Jestyna—she'd got away too. "Cecilia, take my tail. We need to get out of here."

"I have to find Kuffi and my friends."

"I know. Follow me and hold my tail tight. I'll get you to the Nest." And with that Cecilia grabbed Jestyna's tail and they set off into the dark.

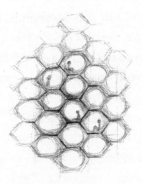

27

Walking on Egg Cells

Cecilia and Jestyna didn't have to travel far to get to the Nest. It was connected to the generator room by a passage of trees on the edge of the Black Forest. She could see a towering structure up ahead and she didn't like the look of it one bit.

The tower was dark and eerie like the ones in fairy tales that characters get trapped in. And Cecilia could see now that that was exactly what the Nest was made for. Cecilia noticed a tiny light pass by her in the darkness they had created by releasing Mr Sparks. It was a firefly—there were lots of them dotted about that were coming from a broken lamp not far off. A fire was being tended to in front of the Nest.

Cecilia knelt down and put her hand in something warm and sticky.

"Yuck, what is that?"

"Droppings, from the surveillance crows," said Jestyna. "Look in the egg cells," she said. "Can you can see your friends? I fear we may need to get closer."

The two of them crept through the darkness, getting a little closer, close enough for Cecilia to see what the Nest really looked like even in the dim light.

It was a huge, lofty tower of egg-shaped containers, each of which acted as a cell to keep its captive imprisoned. They were stacked one on top of another and held in place with wire and cables woven together. Jestyna and Cecilia crouched down trying to work out what to do next when Hunter came over and sniffed them out. Jestyna's back arched and she was about to hiss, but Cecilia grabbed her hand and said, "It's OK, he's on our side. He pressed one of the release buttons to set Mr Sparks free earlier. He helped us out." Jestyna backed down but she was still suspicious. Hunter stood in front of them and gestured for them to hide behind him as bit by bit they inched closer.

Once they were within earshot, Cecilia could see the forms and faces trapped in the transparent egg cells. The Nest was a sad place. Sorrow clung in the air all around it, and the lights around them flickered on and off from time to time like the charge from a dying circuit. Cecilia heard an irritatingly sharp, high-pitched whistle. Hunter's ears pricked up and he stood frozen to attention. And then came the voice:

"Thank you, Hunter. I'll take it from here."

"Cecilia!" screeched Jestyna as she was wrenched away by the scruff of her neck. Hunter bowed his head in shame and dragged himself over to stand beside Jacques d'Or, who patted him on the head. "There's a good boy, now."

Cecilia was beside herself, "*Hunter*? Jestyna, I'm..."

"...Sorry?" said Jacques d'Or. "You'd better be." He was livid, his eyes burning red. "I honestly didn't think you could make things any worse than you already had but now look!" Rage shook his whole body.

"Canines can prove to be such loyal friends, obedient and submissive as well as fearfully strong. They're quite dangerous if not controlled to some degree. Don't you think, Cecilia? Corvus!" Jacques d'Or shouted into the dark spaces above the tower. Two crow-faces flew down like shadows. One of them was the beautiful Aubrey. He handed Jacques d'Or a collar, which he fixed to Hunter's neck and then chained it to the wall of the Nest.

"That will be all, thank you. I'll deal with this little girl and her so-called friends!"

Slowly descending on a pulley was a small wire cage; inside sat Lady-Bird, her wings in tatters and her face hidden.

"You didn't really think that you'd outsmart me did you, silly *little girl*! I'd be wary competing with an opponent I knew so very little about if I were you. Tah-da!" Jacques d'Or sang, gesturing towards an egg shape being rolled along the ground. Cecilia could see Luke inside it.

"Bring him here so she can get a good look at her *friend*," said Jacques d'Or. "He'll make a splendid addition to my Nest, don't you think?"

Luke banged on the wall of the egg cell he was trapped inside, but Cecilia couldn't hear a word he was saying.

"So you recognise this guy?" Jacques d'Or continued. "But... what about this one?"

A second egg cell was rolled out before her and brought to a standstill next to Luke's. Kuffi sat inside it; he pressed his furry hand up to the casing as if to say hello.

"Your old buddy pal, Koof!" Jacques d'Or barked the words. "It looks like you've scored a hat trick. And just to top it off... can we reveal the bonus prize?" he screamed, clapping his wings together.

A figure was dragged in along the dirt and plonked down at Cecilia's feet. She didn't recognise her at first, so many of her feathers had been plucked out.

"Do you know who this is? It's the one and only Madame Midnight! A little extra something just for me! Well, isn't this fun?" Jacques d'Or mused. "No?" He narrowed his eyes. "Do you know what, Cecilia?"

Cecilia shook her head. She could not find the words.

"This is all your fault!" he went on, and at that the Corvus Community let out a searing caw, cackling through the wide open space, sweeping into the air and whooping.

Cecilia stood, petrified and broken.

"He's a bit bedraggled, isn't he? Your old pal Kuffi has refused to eat or drink anything—he believes we will poison him! Now, would I do such a thing?"

Cecilia felt the familiar sensation of her skin crawling as he spoke.

"But don't worry, Cecilia, the show's not over yet! Next," he cawed. "Nothing like a bit of light entertainment! Bring on the menagerie!"

A few of the Divers were brought in. They had been tied up together. Cecilia lost all hope... almost. She counted them up quickly, scanning the group with her eyes. There were two missing—no, one, as she saw Owen was being dragged in from the Black Forest. But Rory, the shark-face, he must've got away, and when was the last time she saw Gaia? She couldn't remember; maybe she hadn't come at all. Cecilia remembered that Doltha had the elemental sphere and she prayed they wouldn't find it. That was not something any of them wanted Jacques d'Or to get his beak around.

"Search them," commanded Jacques d'Or. Just as they began patting down the Divers, there was a commotion high in the rafters of the Nest.

"Something's coming through the walls, boss!" shouted a voice from way up.

"What?" replied Jacques d'Or.

"Something is digging its way through into the roof, sir," another voice called out. "It's the truth, I swear!"

Jacques d'Or looked around at his surrounding Corvus members. Helen was walking over with Marvin and Julius; they all looked furious.

227

"There's something coming through... RIGHT NOW, sir!" Hysteria was breaking out above.

"Helen, go up and see what all the commotion is!" said Jacques d'Or.

"Yes, sir, at once." She bent low and hopped forward once, then twice and took to the air. A few moments later she returned with Rory in her clutches and flung him together with the rest of them.

"I thought something fishy was going on!" said Marvin. Julius patted him on the back and they both burst into fits of laughter.

"The one that got away. Well done! I do love a good scavenger hunt!" Jacques d'Or was in his element. Helen scouted along the line, picking the Divers out in no particular order, and Julius and Marvin finished patting them down. Helen looked annoyed.

"Empty-handed, boss, apart from their weapons, of course," she said, jabbing her fellow Corvus in the side with one of the spears they had confiscated.

Cecilia looked at Doltha; the look on her face told her that everything was going to be OK.

Doltha almost smiled and Jacques d'Or noticed.

"I saw that, flipper. For that *you* can go first."

"What are you going to do to them?" stammered Cecilia, as more of the Corvus Community gathered out of the darkness.

A ruckus broke out from one of the egg cells at the top of the tower. The prisoners had started drumming on their egg cells furiously. There was a loud cracking sound and

Helen pointed out a beam of light coming through the wall where Rory had passed.

"Look!" Helen shouted at Jacques d'Or. "Where's that light coming from?"

Members of the Corvus turned their gaze upwards to see what was happening. A shaft of pure golden light was seeping through a hole high in the cave and shining directly onto the prisoners in the upper egg cells. The light was so strong that the egg cell had begun to crack!

"What on earth is that? Where is it coming from? Aubrey!" shouted Jacques d'Or.

Aubrey leapt out of the shadows into the air but instead of blocking out the light, he began scratching at the hole, moving great clumps of dirt with his beak and hands; bits of the surface of the wall fell away and more light began to fill the caves, revealing scores of black figures high on their perches. One of them seized Aubrey and brought him tumbling down.

"What has got into you, boy!" screeched Jacques d'Or. Countless members of the Corvus Community took to the air and began flapping about the cave in a fluster, trying to black out the light to stop the egg cells from cracking.

Cecilia watched for Jacques d'Or as he ascended towards the bright light, becoming almost invisible, turning away from it, shading his eyes to see. He was utterly blinded; it was like watching someone lose a super power. The Nest was a hive of commotion. Cecilia ran over to Kuffi amid the chaos and pushed his egg cell across the floor and shoved it hard into the tower. It made a cracking sound but didn't break. She looked at him through the cell.

"Stay there, I'll be back," she said.

The Divers were already trying to get loose. Cecilia ran over and found one of the discarded spears, and handed it to Jestyna, who began cutting the others free.

"I need you to break Luke and Kuffi out too," Cecilia shouted against the noise.

Jestyna ran and threw her spear with all her might at the egg cell holding Kuffi and it shattered into a thousand pieces. Then she did the same for Luke.

The Corvus Community were frantic. They didn't know whether to block out the light or to seize the prisoners. Cecilia ran to the base of the tower where Hunter was chained. She looked at him and he did not respond. She began to pull at his collar and she managed to tug it off, but still he did nothing.

"Come on, Hunter!" she screamed into the cacophony of cawing. The message to break out of the egg cells spread up and along the tower like wildfire and soon everyone was gnawing, pecking, scratching and thumping their egg cells all at once. More and more light flooded the space as the members of the Corvus Community pecked at the prisoners, trying to stop them from fleeing.

Jestyna let out a piercing screech and Adriene followed suit, howling high into the rafters, and the remaining members of the Corvus Community that were still on the ground took to the air, petrified. Jacques d'Or was bewildered: he flew out of the streaming light and snatched Cecilia from behind in his arms and took to the air. The Corvus flocked towards the light. It was a pandemonium of Corvus and colours. Jacques d'Or struggled through the fray, higher and higher, Cecilia in his clutches, nearing the highest point of the Nest. Cecilia snatched at his waistcoat pocket, clinging on for dear life as she felt him release his grip and just let her go. She scrambled to grab hold of Jacques d'Or, and when she grasped his whistle the connecting chain snapped off, sending her plummeting towards the ground. As she gathered speed, the air passed through the whistle and she caught a glimpse of Hunter running from his spot below to catch her. Cecilia's body landed on him with such a force that he fell to the ground.

Jacques d'Or raged towards them in a wild fury and Cecilia blew hard on the whistle. Hunter snatched at Jacques d'Or's legs and pulled him out of the air.

"Hunter!" Jacques d'Or screeched. But Hunter gave him no time to speak, bounding off into the Black Forest, dragging Jacques d'Or behind him by the wing, which was locked in his jaw.

Cecilia lay stunned on the ground as the chaos around her began to fade to nothing.

28

Quite a Tumble

When Cecilia woke up, she was battered and bruised but surrounded by many friendly faces gathered around her bed. The room was warm and cosy and she knew instantly that she was back safe in Jasper's cubby. As she stirred she saw Kuffi and jumped into his arms.

"Kuffi!" she cried. "You're all right!"

"I'm fine, little thing. Barely a scratch on me!" he said gently, his whiskers tickling her cheeks.

Kuffi ushered the faces out as soon as Cecilia began to ask questions.

"Where's Luke? Is he OK?"

Kuffi sat on the edge of the bed and began to speak.

"It worked, Cecilia. You brought back the elemental sphere, freed Mr Sparks who has been returned to his home and is happily lighting the lake." Cecilia looked around; it was much brighter.

"When you're ready we will go and see Lady-Bird and Luke..."

A voice harped in. "No need, Koof, I'm right here!" Luke swaggered over to the bed and held up his hand for a high-five.

Kuffi turned back to Cecilia. "When you are up to it, you and I will head back to where we started and see if we can get you home, safe above ground with your family where you belong."

"Wait, what are you saying, Koof?" Luke blurted out.

"Quiet down, both of you, and let me explain. While I was trapped in that egg cell, I discovered I still had in my possession the book you bought at Market Square. You remember? Before things took a turn for the worse?"

"Yes, yes it was a diary," Cecilia added.

"*The Diary of a Button Collector*, in fact. When it was quiet and there were few distractions at the Nest, I would take it out and read through it. I read it from cover to cover. It was fascinating. I learnt a lot about the world—or should I say, universe, in which we live, that I didn't know. Anyway, I digress," said Kuffi, waving away some invisible gnat with his furry hand. "*The Diary of a Button Collector* was written many years ago, so it must have been lost on the heap that is Edwina's enchantingly charming bookstall for quite some time. It is all handwritten so things are quite hard to decipher, but I had quite a bit of time on my hands so I didn't let that put me off. Perhaps that's one of the reasons no one else had wanted to buy it all these years."

Cecilia beamed, already absorbed in the story and so happy that Luke and Kuffi were safe and sitting in front of her.

"The book is a memoir written by Wilma-Rose Newbury. She belonged to a family of explorers and while on a routine expedition to investigate some caves forming on the outskirts of a place called London—if that's how you say it?" Cecilia nodded. "Wilma-Rose recounts that she was scraping at the walls of the cave when she was distracted by a shaft of light coming from within the rock face. She crossed over a fracture in the ground she had already recorded and remarks in her diary that her 'ears popped' due to a change in pressure. Suddenly, she was swallowed up into the tunnels by a sinkhole that opened up beneath her. In her diary she writes of having to shuffle along through an endless darkness."

"Just like me, I had to do that. It was horrible," said Cecilia.

"It does sound familiar, doesn't it?" agreed Kuffi.

"I ran back onto the carriage to get my marble, and I remember my ears popping too, so I guess that's sort of similar to what happened to me."

"Well, Wilma-Rose recalls being delirious and exhausted," Kuffi continued. "She writes of finally coming to an opening and then blacking out. When she came round, she describes introducing herself to an aged, friendly turtle-face called Cuthbert, who helped her navigate the tunnels and who in his time had met with two other 'wanderers' as he liked to call them. They worked tirelessly to find a way to return Wilma-Rose to the surface, and she learnt much about the dwellers and how they lived. In the end Cuthbert and Wilma-Rose discovered that all she had to do to get home was to manually pop her ears and she was back where she started.

"Cecilia, how does one pop one's ears? Is it dangerous?" asked Kuffi.

"You just sort of, hold onto your nose and blow," Cecilia replied.

"That's it?" said Luke.

"Yeah." She nodded.

Cecilia looked at Kuffi and Luke and thought somehow it might be a bit more difficult for them to pop their ears, being as they were put together a bit differently.

Cecilia sat there with her friends, exchanging puzzled looks. She added, "It's something you do to relieve the pressure in your ears when you go deep underground or really high up. It happens where I come from quite often."

Kuffi sat and digested what Cecilia was saying for a moment before he returned to his story. "Ms Wilma-Rose wrote this book for people like you. So you would know how to get home. But she must've forgotten it the last time she left and I think that's because she had her sights set on bigger and brighter things." He paused.

"Like what?" said Luke and Cecilia in unison.

"All in good time," Kuffi said, tucking the book back in his coat pocket. "Let's get back to my cabin and we can test it out there and see if popping your ears will get you home!"

The three of them nodded in agreement. "However, right now, Luke, I think we'd better let the next visitors in or they might burst!"

Two figures had just shown up and were dancing excitedly in the doorway.

Kuffi got up and brushed Cecilia's curly hair away from her forehead. It seemed her two tidy buns had popped out during all the commotion and her wild mane had once again taken on a life of its own. "Be gentle with her," he said softly to the next set of visitors. "She's had quite a tumble."

"In a bit, kiddo!" Luke smiled, swaggering out of the door.

"Later on!" she called out after him.

The two familiar figures of Doltha and Gaia rushed in after Kuffi and Luke had left, and all niceties were dashed aside as they fell on her with open arms.

Doltha went to work checking her over. "You're looking much better. There's colour in your cheeks now," she said, pulling at her ear lobes and inspecting her eyes.

"We are so glad to have you back!" said Gaia.

"I'm glad to be back," Cecilia laughed.

"Oh, you were amazing. Doltha's told me all about it!"

"Gaia, I'm sure Cecilia has had enough drama for today," said Doltha.

"Nonsense, I just want to praise her. She's a hero, Doltha, well, we all are!"

"Glad I could be of service," joked Cecilia. "Though there is something I haven't worked out."

"Oh, what's that?" said Gaia.

"How come they didn't find the elemental sphere on Doltha?" Cecilia was eager to know.

"Ah ha! Because I never had it!" she answered. "Gaia did. In the end we thought it better to send you and the Divers on one part of the mission to act as a distraction whilst also setting Mr Sparks free! Meanwhile, Gaia went off on her own secret mission to Polaris to restore the light to the tunnels and focus its beam directly on the Concave Stadium, which redirects the light all around the tunnels! Clever, huh?"

"And now look," said Gaia.

"It's glorious," said Doltha, stealing her words. Gaia patted them on their backs simultaneously.

"Couldn't have done it without you," she smiled, lifting Cecilia's chin. "You are one brave girl!"

Doltha was clearly becoming quite emotional. Cecilia could see tears forming around the edges of her big friendly eyes and Gaia stepped in. "Come on now, Doltha. I think we'd better go before we are all blubbering messes."

"One last thing before we go," said Doltha, sucking back the tears. "I made you this." Doltha handed Cecilia a small wooden emblem with a crystal gemstone set in it and a pin on the back.

"You're one of us now... a Diver," she said.

"Yes, you'll always be welcome," added Gaia, and with that they left, Doltha pausing in the doorway to wave goodbye.

"All right, Cecilia, you've been given the all clear!"

"Jasper!" Cecilia cried, jumping up and running over to him for a big hug. He patted her on the back as they stood there.

"Good to hear you!" he said. "Now it looks like you're popping off already then?" He nudged her in the side.

"Jasper, are you going to come with me?"

He laughed heartily.

"Heavens, no! The tunnels are my home now. But feel free to come back and visit anytime. We will never forget what you did for us." Cecilia felt the warmth of his words.

Kuffi came over and took Cecilia's hand, and Cecilia waved goodbye.

"Wait for me," called Luke as they entered the secret passage, which was now quite bright and sprouting with moss and small yellow flowers. "There's just one more person to say your goodbyes to and she's waiting for us by the lake."

They walked down Jasper's secret tunnel towards the Concave Stadium and made their way towards the shore of the lake under Polaris. So much had changed in such a short amount of time: the air was alive with song, and exotic fruits hung from lanky vines.

"Here, try this," said Luke, pulling a big round bubble of amber off a nearby stalk.

"What is it?"

"Sweet milk. You drink it," said Luke, biting a hole in the skin and taking a sip. He passed it to Cecilia. "Delicious, huh?"

Cecilia put her lips to it and drained it—the bubble burst.

"Scrummy," she said, licking her lips.

It took a while to walk to the lake. They travelled slowly, taking it all in and chatting, passing the smiling faces of the dwellers that they met along the way. Everyone seemed so happy.

Just as she was about to ask where they might find Lady-Bird, they came to the mound overlooking Polaris and there, sitting peacefully in all her splendour, humming sweetly, was Miss Lady-Bird. Cecilia dashed over to her and tumbled into her arms.

"He's beautiful, isn't he?" said Lady-Bird.

"Who?" said Cecilia, looking out over the sandy surface where a beautiful rainbow glow pulsed.

"Mr Sparks. Of course."

"At one point we thought we were going to have to gather up all the dwellers and fill the lake with tears. We were going to get you to sing and everything," Cecilia said.

"Well, I'm glad it didn't come to that."

Cecilia got up and walked some way over to the edge of the water and touched the surface. She brought her hand away and noticed her fingertips twinkling as she held them up to her face to study them. Luke jogged over and wedged his hands in his pockets.

"Cecilia?" he said softly. "You'll come back and see us sometimes, won't you? I mean, if you can?"

"Of course I will, Luke. I'll find a way. Besides, I owe you a marble." Cecilia felt overwhelmed, both happy and sad at the same time.

"Oh yeah!" said Luke, remembering their deal.

"Goodbye." She waved at Mr Sparks as she and Luke turned back towards their friends where they prepared to part company.

29

Goodbye

Once they'd shared some teary goodbyes, Cecilia and Kuffi walked away from their friends at the lake below Polaris, the sound of people laughing and crying with joy growing further and further away. Now gathering at the water's edge, their faces were wet with tears of happiness. But she didn't feel their happiness. She and Kuffi travelled up the lime line and walked through Market Square. Everything had changed. Kuffi asked if she was hungry or thirsty, if she needed anything, and every time she answered no by silently by shaking her head. So he rested his furry hand on her shoulder instead.

"Kuffi, what will I tell my family when I get home? There will be so many questions. No one will believe me," she said.

"Well then, don't tell them exactly what happened. In many ways it's for the best. The dwellers are a much smaller community of beings compared to where you come from, if Wilma-Rose Newbury's book is anything to go by. We're fragile and belong to a very delicate environment, as you can see. We need to be kept safe. The secrets you have learnt about this place and us, they need to stay down here with us where they belong. We can't have hundreds of wanderers 'popping' down whenever the mood takes them. But you know, you can always write it all down, like Wilma-Rose did, just for you, so you don't forget! Then you can always tell that story to people and they'll know it well and it will be part of their experience—but without ever realising it was real and that it actually happened to you."

"Maybe that's not such a bad idea," she said, looking at her feet. "Kuffi, do you know how the elemental sphere ended up being my birthday present?" Cecilia asked.

"Yes, I've been thinking about that. And it seems Wilma-Rose Newbury took it with her just before she popped home the last time. In her final diary entry she writes of wanting to take something back with her to prove the existence of the tunnels, something special. A new discovery that would make her famous. I don't think she realised the effect it would have on those that dwell here. And it seems like she must have taken the elemental sphere as proof, which had a monumental effect on the lives of the dwellers, as we now know. She did, however, forget her diary, which I dare say is a stroke of luck for us!"

They reached Kuffi's grand entrance and she recognised it right away. It felt like she had only been there a few hours ago.

"It will be much easier for me to catch up on my reading now," Kuffi remarked as they walked into the cabin, which was much brighter.

Kuffi sat in his chair and reached into his pocket and pulled out Wilma-Rose Newbury's diary. "It's time for you to go home," he said. "Have you got all your things? It says to make sure you have everything you want to take with you."

Cecilia opened her rucksack and took out her coat and put it on.

"Right. That's better," she said, sitting back down.

Kuffi flicked through the book and read aloud. Cecilia hugged her rucksack tight to her like a cushion.

"You'd better put that rucksack on," said Kuffi.

Cecilia sat forward and put her arms through the loops, then settled back into her spot.

"Wilma-Rose says to travel back through the tunnels, simply pop your ears."

Kuffi leant forward in his chair.

"Are you ready, little thing?" he asked.

"I'm going to miss you..." she replied.

"Yes. The feeling is a shared one."

Cecilia put her thumb and forefinger on her nose, closed her eyes and swallowed hard, and her ears went *pop*!

30

Hanging in the Balance

Cecilia's eyes were firmly stuck together. She could feel a gentle rocking motion wobbling her from side to side. But she didn't dare to open her eyes right away; she liked the dark these days. One good thing she had learnt was that the darkness didn't frighten her any more. It wasn't suffocating or empty. Living among the dwellers had taught her that the darkness wasn't always lonely or dangerous either. Although it was full of uncertainty, it was also full of promise and excitement. She knew at that moment that she would always carry a bit of darkness around with her.

Cecilia smiled to herself and when she felt ready, she opened her eyes and found she was standing in the same empty train carriage that had left her in the tunnels. It was moving along steadily. For a moment it was hard for Cecilia to believe that she was back where she started after such a sensational journey. Yes, it had been treacherous at times, but having been through it she knew it was something she would never forget. She checked herself over and found she was still wearing the deepsuit the Divers had given her. She could feel the weight of the rucksack they had bought with their winnings from Mrs Hoots' Haberdashery strapped to her back. She shoved her hands in her buttonless coat, feeling around inside her pocket, and there along with the sticky Cherry Drop wrappers was the badge Doltha had gifted her and... there was something else. It was the whistle that had saved her life! How did that get there, she wondered.

"OK," she said aloud to herself. "Mum, Dad and Hester will be worried sick." With that the train paused. Not again, she thought. It just sat there in the tunnel like it had done the last time. She walked up to the door between the carriages, the ones you hardly ever see anyone go through. She went through one, then she ran through the carriage and passed through the next and the next and the next until she was standing in front of the train driver's door.

Cecilia knocked three times. Three knocks were returned and the door swung open.

"What are you doing here?" said a jolly voice. "Get stuck in the loop, did you?" He chuckled to himself. "Don't worry, it happens every now and then. People forget to get off, or they're too slow getting their bits together, or they fall asleep and miss their chance. We have to turn the train around, you see, so we take it round a big, deep loop."

"Cool," Cecilia said slowly.

"I'm Tarquin," said the train driver, holding out his hand. "Come and sit up front. We will be back at Kennington in just a minute."

"Thanks, Tarquin. I'm Cecilia," she said softly.

"Wait a second. Cecilia Hudson-Gray? I got a call on the radio about an hour ago to keep an eye out for you! And here you were all along, turning around in the tunnels!" He slapped his leg. "Well, I'll be darned. I'll let them know I've found you and we are bringing you in."

Looking out of the front window, Cecilia watched a crescent of light grow into a wide open mouth, revealing the tiny figures of people standing on the platform. The train stopped and Tarquin wished her the best of luck as the station manager held the train to talk to him and told Cecilia to take a seat.

Cecilia jumped off the train and sat quietly on the wooden bench, watching passers-by until the station manager was ready to take her back to the ticket hall.

"Right then, miss, let's get you back where you belong."

They waited in the office for her family and the police to arrive but she didn't have to wait long. Cecilia saw them outside the glass, jumped up and rushed out of the door and into the arms of her family as first her mum burst into tears, then Hester and finally her dad.

"Where have you been?" Hester shouted. "You just vanished!"

"Apparently you got stuck on a train they were turning around in the loop," her dad informed her.

"We've been waiting for you for hours. Obviously, we've been worried stupid..."

"How long have I been gone?" Cecilia asked.

Her mum pulled up her sleeve and looked at her watch. "Gosh, just coming up to twelve hours. It's almost ten o'clock!"

"An hour for every year of your life!" Hester mused. "Can we go home now?"

"We can go when the police say so. We're just waiting for them to give us the go ahead," said her mum. Cecilia's dad kept patting her on the head.

"Yeah! The police are here and everything!" said Hester. "They thought you'd been abducted by aliens," she said creepily but Cecilia could tell she'd been crying a lot. She grabbed Hester and gave her a hug.

"Missed you. Wish I'd had you with me, I think you'd have had a good time, funnily enough!"

Hester hugged her back tightly.

"It's not the same without you either, really boring," Hester said as she pulled away.

"Well, it's good to know you weren't abducted by aliens," said Cecilia's mum. "We knew you were on the train. Because we all saw you get whisked away on it. But they worried you'd got off somewhere or something. Because you were gone an abnormally long time."

"They thought you might have got off randomly, thinking you were at a station or something, but they were a bit vague about the details," Cecilia's dad added.

"That made things worse. I kept thinking maybe you'd got lost in some old dark tunnels!" said Mum.

"Well..." said Cecilia.

"You didn't," said Hester, finishing her sentence.

"No, because here you are!" said her dad, giving her a big squeeze.

"And there's still some of your birthday left—although it is quite late."

"Can we go home, just get a pizza or something?" said Cecilia.

"PIZZA! Yes! I'm hungry!" Hester chirped.

"Are you OK, darling? I mean, really?" asked her mum, kissing her on the cheeks and looking deep into her eyes the way only a mum can.

"I am absolutely fine. Just a bit tired and hungry."

"OK. Well, your dad and I will have a chat with the manager and the police. You guys sit on that bench over there while we sort this out and then we will get something to eat, OK?"

"Great," said Cecilia.

Hester and Cecilia sat side by side on a wooden bench while their parents talked to the authorities. Her Mum and Dad kept looking over and smiling.

"Where did you get that rucksack?" asked Hester.

"Oh, I... was wearing it earlier. Didn't you notice?"

"No, you weren't. I remember. And what are you wearing

under your coat?" she said, smoothing her hand over the fuzzy texture of the deepsuit. "Awww, it's all velvety!" Hester smiled.

"Yeah... Charity shop," Cecilia fibbed.

"But you were wearing jeans earlier," said Hester.

"Well, you can't always believe everything you see, can you, kiddo?"

"Kiddo?" she said, scrunching up her nose.

"Right then, kids. Pizza it is!" said her dad, rubbing his hands together. Hester immediately dropped the conversation and jumped to her feet.

"Turns out they took your train for a spring clean or something, that's why it took so much longer to turn round. The person who was sprucing up the insides swears you weren't in there though."

Cecilia and her dad dropped back as Hester skipped ahead holding their mum's hand.

"Must've been quite a scary adventure?" asked her dad.

"Yeah, it was pretty lonely and boring, but all that matters is that I'm back with you guys now," shrugged Cecilia as she found the whistle in her pocket and held it tight in her hand. She linked her dad's arm with her free arm.

"Were you in the pitch dark the whole time?" Her dad looked anxiously at Cecilia.

Cecilia turned to him and said with a serene smile dancing about her mouth, "Yes, pretty much, but you know me, Dad. I'm not afraid of a little bit of darkness."

AVAILABLE AND COMING SOON
FROM PUSHKIN CHILDREN'S BOOKS

We created Pushkin Children's Books to share tales from different languages and cultures with younger readers, and to open the door to the wide, colourful worlds these stories offer.

From picture books and adventure stories to fairy tales and classics, and from fifty-year-old bestsellers to current huge successes abroad, the books on the Pushkin Children's list reflect the very best stories from around the world, for our most discerning readers of all: children.

THE MURDERER'S APE
THE LEGEND OF SALLY JONES
Jakob Wegelius

LAMPIE
Annet Schaap

BOY 87
LOST
Ele Fountain

THE LETTER FOR THE KING
THE SECRETS OF THE WILD WOOD
THE SONG OF SEVEN
THE GOLDSMITH AND THE MASTER THIEF
Tonke Dragt

RED STARS
Davide Morosinotto

WHEN LIFE GIVES YOU MANGOES
Kereen Getten

THE MISSING BARBEGAZZI
THE HUNGRY GHOST
H.S. Norup

THE TUNNELS BELOW
Nadine Wild-Palmer

DUNCAN VERSUS THE GOOGLEYS
Kate Milner

SCHOOL FOR NOBODIES
Susie Bower

THE DEAD WORLD OF LANTHORNE GHULES
Gerald Killingworth